# Midnight
## In The Shadows

Timothy A. Bramlett

authorHOUSE®

*AuthorHouse™*
*1663 Liberty Drive Bloomington, IN 47403*
*www.authorhouse.com Phone: 1-800-839-8640*

*Published by AuthorHouse  7/3/2012*

*ISBN: 978-1-4772-1324-7 (sc)*
*ISBN: 978-1-4772-1323-0 (dj)*
*ISBN: 978-1-4772-1322-3 (e)*

*Library of Congress Control Number: 2012910343*

*This book is dedicated to my wife and best friend, Sharon Bramlett, who taught me that most of the problems in life are just bumps in the road.*

# Contents

# *Preface*

The following short stories represent a raucous romp through the bizarre avenues of science and fantasy. With a touch of noir, splashed with science fiction, and doused with a bit of humor, these stories take the reader on a journey into the dark back alleys of imagination. Whether it's cheap cologne and expensive cigars or expensive cologne and cheap suits, the reader will enjoy the twists and turns that each story makes.

It is also the introduction of Matt Starr, space detective. His association with Sharkey and the Space Pirates will appear in several stories. His visitation, along with your curiosity, will transport you through the vast recesses of deep space and beyond.

Some of the stories were from dreams I have had. All the stories provide lessons to be learned along with a touch of the supernatural that attaches itself to your imagination. One story in particular, *A Visit to Skytropolis*, was made into a children's illustrated book. The opening story, *The Red Giant*, was published in a magazine.

And as always, my stories, although basically serious in nature, will be dispersed with a generous supply of humor. Seriousness is all well and good and has its place in our lives but humor keeps us from becoming too sober. So, with all seriousness aside, I hope you enjoy these stories I wrote especially for you.

-Timothy A. Bramlett

# Chapter 1

# The Red Giant

*D*r. Bernie Hogan's tiny satellite sped away from Earth's gravitational pull at 25,000 miles per hour, heading toward the Alpha Centauri star system. It was the last productive act from the planet Earth before it and Dr. Hogan both were engulfed in a giant red envelope. His satellite was named the *Dove* and was a personal project that punctuated years of amateur rocket research. He was determined to send a space probe into orbit around the Earth, but when it became obvious that the end of the human race was near, he frantically worked on a more powerful and improved version that would go far into deep space. The hope was that it would be discovered by aliens from another planet.

"It's kind of like keeping the memory of the planet alive," he would say to himself. Dr. Hogan was proud of his space probe and had painted its name on the side along with the words, *'To a home on God's celestial shore,'* taken from the hymn *I'll Fly Away*.

The final phase of humanity's existence was dependent on the newly formed red giant, also known as the sun. It became the executioner for all that the Earth had been for its long and storied existence. Soon, the red menace would engulf all of the solar system and each of its planets would become a scorched, lifeless, cremated remnant of its former self. The Jovian planets, also known as Jupiter, Saturn, Uranus, and Neptune, were made up primarily of gasses, and would be reduced to a small inner solid core, a fraction of their former size.

The sun had been the life blood of Earth for billions of years but due to its exhausted hydrogen supply, the star began losing its mass and thus the gravity that held it together. As it cooled, it took on a reddish appearance, expanded outward and with its still intense heat, began to cook the planets.

Mercury was, of course, the first to go as it became a glowing, molten sea of hot lava. Venus was next as its clouds were burned away, exposing its cratered, lifeless surface. It eventually exploded from the tremendous pressure that had built up inside its liquid core.

Earth's turn came as the life-giving atmosphere rich in oxygen was burned away. Plant and animal species methodically began to die out and what was lucky or unlucky to be left was destroyed by either the lack of oxygen or intense heat as even the oceans eventually began to boil. The red halo would creep outward, taking with it Mars, then Jupiter,

Saturn, Uranus Neptune, and finally tiny Pluto, which was innocently minding its business as the outer outpost of the solar system, having suffered the humiliation of being demoted to a minor planet. It would, however, have the last laugh as it would be the final planet to survive before its turn came for conflagration.

Dr. Hogan was one of the last humans to walk on the Earth and during his last days was able to get his rocket ship ready for its journey. Having to use his oxygen generators and living deep below the surface, he held out longer than most people and made rare trips to the top. He still kept records of the surface temperature, oxygen levels, humidity, and other readings that would be of no use to anyone on Earth.

Soon, however, even his insulated world began to fail and he knew the end was close. He struggled to the surface and in the intense heat, pushed the button that sent his rocket soaring into space. In only a few short hours, Dr. Hogan was gone, another victim of the evolutionary process of stars. The last words from his lips before he suffocated were, "I wonder if this is how the dinosaurs felt?"

Someone had written a short poem just hours before Dr. Hogan's death, that read:

> 'The stars in the heavens shall come and go,
> Like all that's graced upon the eye,
> The eastern star that shines so bright,
> Shall be the same to dim in the west and die.'

The *Dove's* launch was perfect and it reached escape velocity of 25,000 miles per hour. It was heading out into space toward Alpha Centauri, the sun's nearest star neighbor, just as Dr. Hogan had planned.

As the Earth continued to cook from the increasing heat and gasses of the sun, the *Dove* passed the planet Mars in about six months and then pierced its way through the asteroid belt. In another year and a half it passed Jupiter's orbit. Four years into its trek it journeyed close to the beautiful planet of Saturn with its majestic rings.

In nine total years it was crossing Uranus' orbit and when it reached sweet sixteen it had come close to Neptune. The *Dove* then entered the Kuiper belt where 'short period' comets reside. Being made mainly of ice, they would also fall prey to the expanding red giant and would eventually melt, turning into gasses.

Finally, the *Dove* reached Pluto in twenty-five years and if it had eyes, it could have seen Pluto's barren, eerily lit surface that resembled the

Moon. But now even Pluto's had a reddish tint from the glow that was moving closer to the outskirts of the solar system.

As the *Dove* left the planetary neighborhood, it entered an area known as the Oort Cloud, a region with millions of orbiting rocks. Ordinarily some of them would have become long period comets, thrown out of orbit by the gravity of the giant planets such as Neptune and Uranus. This would have caused them to hurtle toward the sun in elliptical orbits, seen only once by Earthlings, then lost forever in the vastness of outer space. However, even they were not immune to the giant red fiery glow of the sun's changing structure, as most would be engulfed in heat or thrown far into space by the powerful solar wind to explore their own changing future.

As it left the Oort Cloud region, the *Dove* began its slow, quiet journey through deep space, spending thousands of quiet and peaceful years moving toward Alpha Centauri, the nearest star to the sun, 4.3 light years away. Carrying its nostalgic cargo along with its dead solar powered batteries, the *Dove* had long since become an inert, lifeless, silent, projectile, hurtling through space in a quiet world of serene emptiness. It was no longer sending out a beacon and would have to be discovered and retrieved by some advanced civilization in order for the legacy of planet

Earth to be remembered. The odds of this seemed remote but with new and advanced spaceships scattered throughout the galaxy, they could detect any object of comparable size, and since the *Dove* was metallic, the chances of its discovery were even greater.

The *Dove* had a hastily assembled and rather unorganized cache of tapes, pictures, and records, that chronicled the history of the planet called Earth, in case anyone in the far reaches of the galaxy really cared. Some of Dr. Hogan's hair was also included, along with hair of several other people. His thinking that some advanced civilization might one day clone his DNA and create a replica of himself and the others, and thus perpetuate the human race.

This scenario of dying but inhabited planets had been, unfortunately, played out many times before and was nothing new in the galaxy. Actually, antiquated spacecraft like the *Dove* had often been found by space patrols from other worlds.

For the next 100,000 years, the *Dove* flew silently through space, getting ever closer to that magic neighboring star called Alpha Centauri. With virtually nothing in between but stars, nebulae, and a few distant galaxies, it was a rather uneventful trip. However, the sealed capsule kept everything intact and nothing decayed, discolored, or rotted. In the dry vacuum of space all the contents were preserved just as if it had left the day before.

Dr. Hogan's calculations were incredibly accurate as the target star became brighter and brighter. Soon, there were shadows within the capsule itself from a small window that he had installed. It was from here that a camera had been carefully placed, which took pictures of Earth as it rocketed outward bound, into the stratosphere and beyond. This would, he thought, help explain the capsule's existence as it escaped a dying planet and a chaotic and convulsing solar system.

With Alpha Centauri becoming a bright magnitude star now, a miracle took place within the *Dove*. The sensitive photo electric cells suddenly came to life and a red light began to glow, indicating that the batteries were being recharged.

In a period of only six hours, the radio was ready to start transmitting again. Dr. Hogan's little capsule awoke from its deep sleep, shook off the cobwebs, and began to speak in its own way. The message Dr. Hogan recorded in his own voice, repeated over and over again: "Hello from planet Earth. We are in grave trouble. Planet burning up from the heat of the sun. No chance for survival." This message played for five minutes, rested for one hour, then repeated. This procedure continued as long as the cells and the transmitter would continue to function.

Steady Morse code signals were also transmitted across outer space in several frequencies that were designed to draw attention to the *Dove*. Inside the capsule was an explanation of each word that he spoke and each Morse code letter, matching them with pictures and words that would explain exactly what he was talking about. He gave the time of the *Dove*'s departure coordinated with an internal clock. He explained Earth's relationship to the other stars in the galaxy, pinpointing its location. It would be simple for anyone to see the pictures and match the words. And although it was too late to save the Earth, the memory would live on. Perhaps a distant neighboring civilization would erect a monument in the memory of Earth and someday place it on its burned out remains. They might even create a museum that would explain the beginning and end of a world. What a glorious tribute to a planet and star that lived out their usefulness.

The *Dove* sailed past two planets, then a third, but there was no indication that Dr. Hogan's words were being heard. As the capsule crossed the Alpha Centauri solar system, the same words kept repeating at one hour intervals. A steady radio signal poured into space but fell on deaf ears. In a few years, the *Dove* had traversed its intended destination and had not been seen or detected. Either there were no humanoids below or they were not scientifically sophisticated enough to either detect or intercept the tiny capsule.

As the *Dove* pulled away from Alpha Centauri, the starlight dimmed and the capsule became dark again. The batteries died out and the photo electric cells ceased to gather light rays. The only hope for Earth's memory became quiet again in the darkness of outer space. As it moved quietly at 25,000 miles per hour, the capsule was dormant again inside, waiting for something else to happen. A popular conception is that it could travel for eternity without detection, for the universe is of infinite proportions with incredible distances between stars. However, the '*law of eternal probability*' refutes this theory by stating that '*no matter how eternally large the odds are against a given occurrence, it will inevitably occur.*'

In approximately 900,000 more years, the *Dove* had traveled 36 light years, or 219 trillion miles. It had been another quiet journey, uneventful except for a close call with a couple of asteroids that came within a mile or so of the capsule. The only thing that changed were the relative position of the visible stars, which shifted during the journey.

The records remained intact and explained the history of Earth from start to finish - a history that stretched for billions of years, from a theorized 'big bang' to the red giant. From one-celled plants and animals to the humans. It covered the great civilizations such as the Incas and the Aztecs. Dr. Hogan included libraries of information, condensed on microfilm about the history of the human race including wars, great scientists, inventions, sporting events, religion, medicine, ecology, and every other conceivable subject. From books by great minds to music from the most brilliant composers. From the most incredible works of art to architectural masterpieces. The whole history of the world was contained in one small capsule, condensed and hermetically sealed into a package suitable for a timeless trip across the galaxy, and maybe the universe.

The next destination for the *Dove* was the double star system called Castor and Pollux. They formed the "twins" in the constellation Gemini. Pollux was the closer of the two and Dr. Hogan's capsule was traveling almost directly toward it on a collision course. This was, of course, totally unplanned and would not have occurred at all had it not been for gravitational pull from Alpha Centauri which skewed the Dove away from its straight course and vectored it toward Pollux.

This proved to be serendipitously advantageous for the *Dove*'s potentially continued survival. As it neared Pollux, the starlight activated the photo electric cells, which once again fed the batteries with life giving electricity. The *Dove*'s brain sprang to life again, spewing out the same messages. Maybe this time it would be heard.

Off in the distance was an inhabited planet called *Celaquan*, orbiting the star Pollux. On its surface was an advanced civilization, far more that than humans ever were on Earth. They heard the call of the *Dove* and immediately relayed it to a nearby Space Patrol ship called '*GemSP-6*.' And just like that, the Space Patrol drew a bead on the tiny capsule and zeroed in on its quarry to investigate.

Antiquated spacecraft like the *Dove* had often been found by space patrols from other worlds. The Reclamation Division of the U.S.S.A., or *Unified Space Security Administration*, had collected thousands of these derelict travelers with much the same information as the rest. Stored in a warehouse called Outpost 505, most had simply been put away. At first it was interesting to open up these timeless crypts but after a few thousand, it was decided just to store them for a while. They *would be* assigned a file number and after a period of approximately one hundred Earth years, and if no one claimed them, they were disposed of by sending them into the nearby white star called Castor-4 for incineration. Each sector of the galaxy had thousands of these outposts for so-called space junk reclamation projects. A sign on the door of the main office in the Pollux sector read '*It's your galaxy, let's keep it clean.*'

Late that afternoon as GemSP-6 closed in and began listening to the *Dove*, something seemed unique and special about the capsule's recorded message. It appeared that it might have some information that could be useful to the history of the galaxy. A curious message describing a premature nova that occurred about a million years ago coincided with an event 36 light years away.

"I think we may have something interesting here," the captain of the reclamation ship exclaimed.

"Bring it back for analysis," a voice answered.

As they hauled the *Dove* back to the laboratory, they opened up the hatch, checked for deadly bacteria and viruses, cleared it for inspection, retrieved and examined some of the materials.

"Amazing," the director of the analysis team stated, "This explains the nova that was reported so long ago. A star suddenly flared into a red giant in that region."

The Lieutenant added, "If only they had known about the new Hydrogen Injection technique. Their star could have been revitalized by the introduction of hydrogen into its core creating nuclear fusion. It would have saved their star and the inhabitants of their planet would have been saved."

"Anything you want to keep?" the pilot of the GemSP-6 stated as he visually scanned the contents of the *Dove*. He looked at his watch and realized that he was supposed to take his kids to the ballgame later in the evening. He didn't want to be late.

"Not really," the director answered as he hastily shuffled through a few of the various remnants. "It's getting late and I'm tired. We'll store the capsule in the archives with the others."

As the technicians were putting the contents back into the capsule, a wad of hair fell out of one of the boxes onto the floor.

"What's this?" the Lieutenant asked.

"Why, it looks like hair," the director added.

After reading and deciphering an attached document, a technician explained, "The builder of this primitive spacecraft had a message that we should use the genetic material from this hair and clone a duplicate of himself and others to perpetuate the Earthling population."

"What do you know," the pilot answered with a chuckle. "Another one of those." They had a good laugh and prepared the *Dove* for storage.

"We'll put the hair inside the capsule with the rest of its contents," the director said. "We don't need any more DNA. We've got plenty already to experiment with." He pointed to a box on the laboratory table where a mixture of different types of alien hair was stored.

As they started to put the items back into the capsule, a few strands of hair fell out and landed on the floor, unnoticed.

The *Dove* was closed and sealed and given the designation 06-9974-443C and was docked to be sent to Outpost 505 in the morning.

Later that evening after the technicians and scientists had gone home, a janitor was cleaning up the area. He had noticed the loose hair lying on the floor and picked it up. "It must have fallen off the table," he said to himself. He placed the hair from Earth into the container labeled 'to be cloned.'

The laws of chance and design that shaped the creation and development of the universe, the galaxies, the stars, the planet Earth, and the tiny bit of hair with its DNA, would be set into motion by the same invisible hands of fate. The hair would wait its turn in some white sterile alien laboratory many light years away to be cloned, somehow defeating

the odds and perpetuating Earth's human race after all.

As for the *Dove*, it sat quietly for one hundred years with many other similar capsules, each with its own story to tell, each with a world of information. Of course no one claimed the *Dove* and it was eventually sent, along with its contents, into the fiery furnace known as Castor-4 for incineration.

But on its journey toward this hot star, something happened inside the *Dove* as it was launched by a pilot vehicle. The vibration caused a tape player to become activated-something that the aliens had hastily overlooked. It began to play the song 'Whiter Shade of Pale' as it hurtled toward the bright sun. It was one of Dr. Hogan's favorite songs, one that he thought would be representative of the music on Earth. 'Aliens from other planets needed to hear some music from Earth,' he had thought to himself when he programmed the song into the tape player many years ago.

So this became the last words from Earth, un-heard by anyone but still existing. And as the capsule got closer to Castor-4, it was destroyed in its entirety by the searing heat, except the strands of hair that were left at the laboratory. The *Dove* was joined by the other archival planetary derelicts that lived out their usefulness and became just another forgotten chapter in the history of the universe.

As for Dr. Hogan's dream, it seemed to have indeed made its way to a home on God's celestial shore.

# Chapter 2

# Just A Bum

Reginald Drake sat comfortably in the back seat of his limousine as he peered out the tinted window, looking down at the homeless people on the sidewalk. 'They should get a job,' he thought to himself. 'Such a pity, clogging up the city streets like that. No wonder my taxes are so high.' He continued to read the financial section of the paper as Thomas, his chauffer, drove them down Bleaker Street, one of the seedier parts of town.

"I don't feel too comfortable going down this street," Thomas said to Mr. Drake, using the intercom.

"Ah, don't worry, Thomas," Reginald answered. "We'll be through here in a couple of minutes. Just keep the doors locked. It's a shame they had to detour traffic because of an accident. People should be more careful. They're holding me up for an important meeting. There goes my tax money again. They should make these idiots pay for inconveniencing important people."

"Right, sir," Thomas added as he squinted and peeked back at Reginald through the rear view mirror.

They continued on down the part of town known disrespectfully as "Skid Row," when suddenly Reginald heard a loud bump underneath the car.

"What was that?" he called up to Thomas, who had already begun slowing down.

"I don't know. We'd better pull over and look."

Reginald's biggest fear was that they had run over some derelict wino that passed out and slid under the wheels. 'That would really put us behind schedule,' he thought.

"What a terrible place to pull over," he announced to Thomas. "Why couldn't it have been on Broadway or Fifth Avenue?"

Both Thomas and Reginald got out of the car and noticed that they had a flat tire. "Drat the luck," Reginald said as he instructed Thomas to get back in and keep driving. This area of town was dirty and shady and reeked of odors that Reginald had never smelled before.

"Very well, sir," Thomas said hastily as they locked themselves back in the limo. They continued on but slower than before.

They had traveled only a block when Reginald noticed something disturbing as he shifted in his patent leather seat.

"I've misplaced my wallet!" he said with panic in his voice over the intercom. "It must have fallen out of my pocket when we got out. We must go back. I have some valuable documents, credit cards, and cash. All kinds of things."

"We can't go back," Thomas stated, almost relieved. "It's a one way street."

"Then stop the car. I'll walk back. It's only a block. You stay here and wait for me. And don't leave till I get back."

Thomas pulled over and let Reginald out of the car.

"Be careful, sir." Thomas pleaded.

Reginald backtracked until he had gotten to where he thought they had stopped. Looking around the gutter and sidewalk, he surmised that his wallet was not there. "Some bum probably stole it," he said to himself. "I guess he'll be having a great day."

"Lost something, sir?" a voice behind him asked politely.

Turning around, Reginald noticed a black man, dressed in ragged pants and shirt, unshaven and dirty. His shoes were badly scuffed and hadn't seen any polish in many a day.

"Uh, I lost my wallet," Reginald stated as he backed away from the gentleman.

"Let me help you look for it," the man said.

"That's ok," Reginald responded dejectedly. "It's not here. I guess somebody took it."

The man noticed Reginald's silk suit and Italian shoes, although could not identify them as such. He only knew they were not what he was used to seeing in this neighborhood.

"Looks like rain," the man said to Reginald. Sure enough, the sky had darkened and Reginald could feel a sprinkle. The temperature had dropped somewhat and he could also feel a chill in the air.

"Go ahead," Chester said to Reginald. "It's okay, take a drink, we got another bottle hidden under a rock."

He took a sip and knew it wasn't Chateau Le Fleur. It was a cheap but rather refreshing wine.

From behind a cardboard crate came Buster, the terrier mix dog to greet Reginald.

"He's our warning system," Roberto said. "If anyone comes near, he lets us know."

"He also keeps rats away," Chester added with a laugh.

"Rats?" Reginald said with concern.

Reginald took another sip of wine and before long, the six pals were sharing stories about everything except how they happened to be under a bridge. They were careful not to pry in each other's private lives or ask questions about their past.

In a while, the wine and fish made them all feel pretty good. "Alvin?" Chester asked, "What would you do if money grew on trees?"

It was almost like a rehearsed version of the classic song. Alvin responded with, "If money grew on trees, I'd have a fortune blowing in the breeze."

"If money grew on trees," Slick philosophized as he picked his teeth with a wooded toothpick he'd fashioned from a sliver of driftwood, "I'd have a toy factory and build Clunkers."

"What are clunkers?" Reginald curiously asked.

"Clunkers, my good man," Slick added, "would be toy cars. Not new ones but old, worn out types. You know, like an '86 Oldsmobile. It would have dents, rust spots, and paint issues. I think people would buy them. That's how I'd make my fortune."

"Hmmm," Reginald mused, "not a bad idea. With the right kind of marketing, who knows."

Soon, as the time passed, Reginald started getting sleepy as did the rest of the motley crew. One by one, they began lying down on the cold ground, carpeted only by old brown cardboard. They covered themselves with moth eaten second hand blankets as close to the smoldering barrel as they could get. Buster curled up with ears perked, ready to detect any intruding movement.

Reginald lay down and thought a little rest wouldn't hurt. He watched the flickering flames as they danced above the barrel and heard the gentle river. He fought sleep but the crickets finally lulled him to sleep.

In a sleep that could have been eight hours or a thousand years,

Reginald had never slept so well. It was as if the world itself was passing by with all its troubles and woes and leaving him alone with his new found friends.

And then, suddenly, Reginald woke up with a start. The night passed in the blink of an eye and now It was daylight. He could hear traffic moving frantically overhead. All of the fellows were still asleep except for Chester, who had a fishing pole in the water, carefully watching for a bite. Buster was right beside him, ever alert. Reginald walked over to them.

"Caught anything yet?" he asked sleepily.

"Nothing yet," Chester said politely. "But it's early yet. How'd you sleep?"

"Like a baby. Didn't stir all night."

"We got a good place here," Chester said. "I hope they don't run us off. They do that sometimes, you know. We should be fine here for a few days anyway. Then we just find somewhere else to go."

Then suddenly, like a bolt from the blue, Reginald realized that people would be looking for him. They were probably combing the streets right now. He needed to get going.

"I'm going for a walk," he told Chester as the rest of his friends slept in. Buster was alertly sniffing around.

"See 'ya later," Chester answered as he lifted his hand to wave, not taking his eyes off the fishing line.

Reginald scurried up the hill and found the top of the bridge. Cars were zooming by, heading to some unknown destination, filled with commuters and people in suits and ties. Some of the people looked down on Reginald as they passed. Some, upon catching a glimpse of him, looked the other way. Others were absorbed in their newspapers as they rode down the road toward their work locations.

He went back down the hill and noticed Chester was still hard at work catching his breakfast. Reggie then turned up the trail and walked past the Rodney's Roost, which was fast asleep after a busy night. He found his way to the main road and started briskly walking. Soon, a police car stopped and summoned him over.

"Are you Reginald Drake?" the policeman said after looking at a picture of him.

"Yes," Reginald answered as he stood beside the opened driver's window.

"Are you all okay? We've been looking for you all night."

"I'm fine. I guess I just got sidetracked."

Reginald got into the police car and headed back to his building. When he arrived, an embarrassed chauffeur explained that he had to move the car due to traffic congestion and couldn't stay. He came back later, Thomas explained, but did not see Reginald and contacted the police.

"It's okay, Thomas. I made it just fine. Even made some new friends." He changed clothes but carefully packed away his thrift store finds.

The office was totally awed by his story. At the board of directors meeting that afternoon, Reginald mentioned an idea about a new product he called "Clunkers." The board was enthusiastic about it and work would start immediately.

"I'm starting a special fund for homeless people," Reginald stated as he explained the Clunker idea to the board. The proceeds from this project will go to this cause."

Several days later, Reginald donned his old thrift store clothes and returned to the bridge. He walked underneath to tell the marketing idea to his friends. The old rusty barrel was cold and the place was deserted. Only a few pieces of cardboard and the old fishing pole remained. On the ground were some fish bones and a cigarette butt. There was an empty wine bottle. But something caught his eye as he looked down. It was a wallet. The wallet he had lost. He picked it up and opened it. Everything was there just as he had left it.

"I wonder how my wallet got here?" he said to himself. "And what happened to Chester, Alvin, Slick, and Roberto?"

He then remembered what Chester had said earlier. "We're all just passing through this world."

Reginald spent many days looking for his friends but could never find them. But the Clunker idea came to fruition which he called the Slick Toy Company. It produced millions of dollars which was used for helping homeless people. "I want the homeless to know that some people really do care," Reginald would often say, "even though we're all just passing through this life."

# Chapter 3

# A fly on the Wall

*T*he city apartment complex had a thousand eyes and they were all looking at Harvey Hicks-or at least he felt like they were. Paranoia, maybe? But when he walked down the steps from the fifth floor, he figured they all must have been listening through closed doors, wondering where he was heading, where he'd been, and what he was going to do. His only friend in the apartment, Oscar Thompson greeted him with his usual curiosity, unusual for the apartment house. "Hiya, Harvey. What's happening?"

"Nothing much, Oscar," Harvey answered.

There was really no need for paranoia, for the thousand or so eyes were hiding behind their own problems and certainly they didn't want to get involved with other people's troubles too. 'I mind my own business' was the phrase that most people lived by. It seemed the best way to survive in the asphalt jungle.

Harvey worked at a local package store. He clerked, stocked, and doled out cigarette packs and rang up cases of beer and bottles of wine. He knew every wino by name. He caught shoplifters and sometimes, when they looked poor enough, he didn't say anything and let them go without a fuss.

His was a mundane lifestyle, to say the least, punctuated by his perpetual five o'clock shadow. It seemed to be a permanent fixture on his middle aged face, weather beaten and rough cut. His tousled hair was never neatly combed and his clothes were straight out of the fifties. He lived alone in apartment 506 on the top floor. He came and went without fanfare and like the rest of the residents, was hardly noticed by the others.

His wife left him years ago, perhaps because she couldn't stand his retro compulsive behavior.

Today, however, was a new day. But it was a typical day in New York City. The hustle and bustle of the crowds never ceased to amaze Harvey, for he came from a smaller, rather rural town in Wisconsin. Coming to the city was a choice he didn't completely make on his own, for his wife got a job in a bank and was transferred there. He tagged along and managed to find work, when work could be found. Finally he settled into the life of a clerk. When she left, he stayed on, rather than go back to the old home town, although sometimes he wished he had.

When four o'clock came on this typical August afternoon, Harvey turned over the reins to Bill Thornton, much his junior but still more than capable of handling the shop until the store closed at midnight. Harvey went straight to his apartment and climbed the twelve steps up to the front door, punched in his secret code and let himself in. He walked down the hallway that took exactly fourteen steps to the elevator at the end of the hall, passing by the mail boxes -usually empty except for an occasional bill. He rode up to the fifth floor and put his key into the lock of number 506 and opened the squeaky wooden door.

Inside he entered a small vestibule where he stopped, turned around, and carefully closed and locked his front door with a dead bolt. He turned around to face another door, punched in more secret numbers and went into his apartment. A glowing red light pulsated in the corner of the room. A large computer covered the entire west wall and one of his three desks was covered with envelopes, some of which had "top secret" written on the front. In his room was radio equipment with microphones and several computer screens, displaying curious codes and numbers that changed periodically. A blue light flashed and blinked on a telephone receiver, which Harvey picked up.

"It's about time you got here," the voice said on the other end.

"I was soaking in the hot tub at the YMCA," Harvey responded sarcastically.

"What time does the train arrive today?" the man said on the other side.

"Pink 606," Harvey responded.

"I'm glad we got that cleared up," the man answered.

It was obvious a set of codes they exchanged to be sure they were talking to the right person.

"I need you to meet a lady at the Salty Stork Bar tonight at seven o'clock."

"I'll be there," Harvey responded calmly.

"She's blond, five foot four, medium build, beautiful, and wearing a yellow tee shirt that reads 'NYU' in blue letters. She's also wearing a red garnet ring on her right hand pinkie. Got it?"

"Loud and clear," Harvey answered as he started munching on an oatmeal cookie.

"You'll ask her if you can sit down beside her and she'll answer with 'Only if you can tell me which horse will win race number four tomorrow.' Your answer will be 'Soup Kitchen.' Got it?"

"Right, chief," Harvey answered.

"This will be our last communication for a while. Until further notice you will be working with them." He abruptly hung up on Harvey, terminating the conversation.

Harvey followed orders and prepared for the rendezvous with a mysterious lady wearing a New York University tee shirt. It was going to be an interesting night - maybe.

When six thirty came Harvey left his apartment, locked both doors behind him, and walked the four blocks to the Salty Stork, entering the front door. He looked around through the haze of cigarette smoke and in a couple of minutes spotted the lady across the room. He saw the yellow tee shirt with NYU on the front as the woman sat reading a newspaper. She was wearing a red garnet ring on her right pinkie. 'Must be her,' he thought to himself confidently. 'It's a good thing everybody's not wearing a yellow tee shirt with NYU on it.' He walked over to the table.

"May I sit down?" he asked politely.

"Only if you can tell me the winner of race number four tomorrow," she responded.

"I do believe it will be an old nag named 'Soup Kitchen,'" he retorted.

"Sit down," she said to him cracking a smile, pointing at the chair next to her.

He summoned the waiter and ordered a drink for each of them.

"Your work has been incredible," she said to Harvey. "Your case officer has told me some of the things you've done."

"Thanks," he said sheepishly as he fumbled nervously with his drink, almost flipping his olive out of his martini glass with the stirring stick.

"I'm the CIA operative they've told you about," she said as she took a sip of her martini. She showed him her I.D. card. "Just call me Jane. You're finished with the FBI for a while since you helped bust up the organized crime ring in the city. They told me the walls have ears. How did it all this come about?" she inquired.

He started telling her the whole story. "The walls have ears," Harvey said with a smile. "Interesting way of putting it. You see, I've been working with Latent Audio Residual research for a long time."

"And what are Latent Audio Residuals?" she asked as she checked to see no one else was listening.

"Well," Harvey explained, "When sound or light or any other type of energy source is emitted or produced, it doesn't just disappear. We used to think that sound waves were just absorbed into the atmosphere and vanished. Well, any physicist or chemist can tell you that nothing ever completely disappears. It may change energy forms but never vanishes completely."

"What happens to it?" she asked.

"If it is in an enclosed area, it is absorbed into the walls," Harvey stated. "If you're outside, it may become absorbed in a tree or sidewalk or some other object like a rock or something."

"Interesting," Jane responded, somewhat amazed. "And then what happens?"

"It stays inside the sub atomic structure of the walls as a latent energy source. It can be retrieved using the right technique. It's sort of like putting a finger print onto the wall. All you have to do is dust it and there you have it."

"So how do you retrieve the sound?"

"It's called a Sound Print Integrator, or SPI."

"'Wow," Jane said excitedly, "how appropriate."

"Yes, with the SPI, I can retrieve the sound energy and integrate it into words. When criminals have been in a jail cell or a hideout, I can tell what they have been talking about and the police can nab them."

"And that's how you cracked all those cases for the police and the FBI?" Jane inquired.

"Exactly," Harvey agreed. "All we have to know is where they have been and I come in with my SPI equipment and scan the area."

"What about other sounds that have been in the room?" she asked

"Good question," Harvey explained. "Latent sound exists in levels, sort of like shells of electrons in an atom. The SPI takes the latest sounds and integrates them. The earlier ones are harder to get to but I'm working on it."

"Where is your SPI machine?" Jane asked.

"It's in my apartment. In fact, I have the only one of its kind. The FBI wanted to buy it from me but I told them I didn't want to sell it. They respected my wishes."

"And why don't you want the FBI to have one?"

"Because it could fall into the wrong hands," Harvey stated with concern. "Can you imagine what would happen if criminals got ahold of it?"

"Does that secrecy go for the CIA too?" she asked.

"I'm afraid so," Harvey answered. "I just can't take any chances."

"I understand." Jane said as she finished up her martini. "Another one, Harvey?"

"Sure, why not."

They continued to talk when finally Jane got to the real point of the meeting. "The reason I wanted to talk to you is a matter of national security. As you know the embassies have foreign diplomats that have a lot of secrets that we need to know. Get the picture?"

"Sure do," Harvey said as he crunched on his olive. "You want me to find out what they've been talking about, right?"

"Right," Jane agreed. "The particular embassy is of no concern of yours right now. All we want you to do is to find out what they've been saying about a possible terrorist plot against the United States."

"Why don't you just bug the rooms?" Harvey asked.

"They have ways to detect bugs," Jane explained. "That's why we need you and your machine."

"You can count on me," Harvey said with a burst of patriotism.

"Go to LaGuardia Airport tomorrow morning and catch flight 601 to Washington, D.C. at 9:05 A.M. There will be a ticket for you at the Capitol Airways desk."

They ended their meeting and left the bar. He packed his SPI machine in a briefcase then left his apartment and headed for the airport the next morning.

On his way out of the building, his friend Oscar stopped him. "Where you going in such a hurry, Harv?"

"Got urgent business back home in Wisconsin. I'll be back in a few days."

"Not a sick relative, I hope."

"No, nothing like that, Oscar. Just have to take care of some loose ends."

"Have a nice trip."

Upon landing in Washington, Harvey was met by two secret service officers who escorted him to a car with darkened windows. It was a short trip across the Potomac River to a secret location and up to the top floor where he met with more CIA officials. He was informed that he would be staying there for a few days. His quarters were very comfortable with all the amenities of a triple A class hotel.

"Tomorrow, you'll be dressed like a plumber, Harvey," the man said. "Your briefcase will be with you. You will enter the room and do your thing. We need to know as much as you can tell us about the past three days."

"And that's all there is to it?" Harvey asked.

"For now," the man said. "Those diplomats are scheduled to be at a meeting at 2:00 P.M. this afternoon. About 2:30 we'll take you to a house on New Hampshire Avenue and to the room where they are staying."

"Sounds easy enough," Harvey answered. "I'm glad to help out, especially for national security. But I can't even fix a leaky faucet."

"We're hoping they will leak more important things than a few drips of water," the CIA agent told Harvey.

Soon, Harvey Hicks was at his location. Everything went like clockwork and he was impressed by the CIA's efficiency. "Don't worry," the agent told Harvey, "we'll be outside the door if you need anything." This made him feel more comfortable. He was, however, a bit uneasy about spying on some foreign people's private business.

Harvey entered the room and went right to work. Soon, his Sound Print Integrator was receiving and collating all sorts of data. As it worked, he could hear what sounded like a tape put on high speed, a garbled string of unintelligible sounds resembling a group of mice going after a hunk of cheese. He set the controls for the past three days and it was done in a matter of a few minutes. He exited the room and handed over the disk to the agents. "The faucet is all fixed," Harvey quipped. "Send the bill to my office, please."

"You did good," the agent said. "We'll take you back to your hotel where you will await further instructions."

Later that afternoon, one of the agents entered Harvey's room. "We're depositing $25,000 in your bank account. Just a little token of our appreciation."

"Much obliged," Harvey responded as he thought about the easy money he'd just made in the name of national security. "Anything else I can do for you gentlemen?"

"That's all for now." They shook hands and prepared to return to their quarters.

Soon he was back at his secret apartment with a steak dinner with wine and all the trimmings he could ask for. "Another $25,000 in your bank account," the agent announced as he opened a bottle of fine wine. "Compliments of Uncle Sam."

"I could get used to living like this," Harvey said as he sipped on the wine. "Think I could stay here a while? Fifty thousand dollars and all the great food I can eat."

"Sorry, we can't do that. But I'm sure you will be here again in the near future."

As all good things, it had to end. The next morning the CIA agent announced, "We have a plane ticket for you. We appreciate your help and we'll be calling on you again soon. Have a nice trip back to New York."

Soon, Harvey Hicks landed at LaGuardia Airport and took a taxi back to his apartment. He was due to work at the package store on the night shift that evening. He entered the apartment where Oscar Thompson greeted him, "Hiya, Harvey, have a nice trip to Wisconsin?"

"Uh, sure. It was nice. But I'm glad to be back."

He took the elevator to the fifth floor, went inside and checked his telephone. The blue light was flashing and a voice on the other end said, "Good work, Harvey. You enjoy your evening. I'll be contacting you in a couple of days for another assignment."

Harvey went to work that evening and it was business as usual. Cigarettes, beer, and wine were selling like hotcakes. A fellow picked up a newspaper. He read the headlines to Harvey, "Terrorist threat thwarted. Arrests made in Washington, D.C."

"How do they do that?" the man said as he handed Harvey a dollar for the paper.

"Beats me," Harvey said. "Those CIA and FBI guys are pretty amazing."

# Chapter 4

# Raising the Devil

*I*n the town of Denton, Missouri, all seemed well on that typical and peaceful summer morning in June. And why shouldn't it? The happy and serene community of 2,000 God-fearing citizens went about their usual business on the Sabbath as they always did.

At the Randle house on Wick Street, the day started out with a leisurely but somewhat fancier breakfast than usual This morning's bill of fare included waffles with real New England maple syrup, sausages, apple sauce, and fresh squeezed orange juice. This was followed by a look at the Sunday newspaper with everyone grabbing for their favorite section.

Then it was time for the Sunday morning bathroom traffic jam ritual but in a somewhat orderly fashion as the pecking order was strictly observed.

Julie Randle was first, followed by her husband, Mike, who would often mumble to himself, "Why didn't I have two bath rooms put in when I built this house." As an engineer, he often wondered how such an important detail was omitted when he was helping design the house. The elder child Janet was next and bringing up the rear in the bathroom parade was the younger child, Martin.

Sunday was a day of rest in Denton, for the Lord rested on the Sabbath and so did the citizens of this laid back Missouri town. There would be no lawn mowing, no painting of houses, no plowing of fields, no fixing any mechanical devices, and no gardening. It was a day to sit on the porch with a tall glass of lemonade, visit with friends or neighbors with your feet propped up on the railing, followed by a discussion of the week's events. The only physical activities allowed were swatting flies, cooking meals, or if you under the age of eighteen, a baseball game at the school house field.

As the people filed into church, they were unaware of the changes that were rapidly approaching like a gigantic invisible twister just beyond the horizon on that clear and peaceful day. And what a beautiful day it was. The early summer flowers were blooming like never before. The colors were exquisite and bright. It was like God Himself touched them for the Christian faithful to see and enjoy. But we all know how quickly a flower can fade. One morning it's beautiful and fresh and the next it's wilting and dark, a shadow of its former self. But for now, at least, the sun shone brightly on their town and church and the birds sang cheerfully as they went about their business.

On the marquis in front of the Denton First United Christian Church was a simple synopsis of the sermon of the day- Raising the Devil. A bit unconventional for Reverend James Ferguson but on the wake of a crime wave in the nearby city of Glenville, the good pastor thought it wise to remind his flock of their responsibilities as good Christians and to raise their children accordingly. It was also a good day to remind the members that evil forces inhabit every corner of their lives and that they are in a constant battle against temptation. 'It would be a fire and brimstone sermon,' he thought to himself as he paced in his study, faintly listening to the choir two doors down rehearse the closing hymn, 'Leaning on the Everlasting Arms.'

Although bad crimes had not hit the town of Denton yet and hopefully never would, Pastor Ferguson still felt a need to alert his flock to the dangers of moral decay that lay near the boundaries of this peaceful community. He thought of World War II and the complacency that grasped a lot of Americans as they heard of a far away land called Germany and their comical looking but evil dictator Adolph Hitler. A war that seemed so far away and so non-threatening. So distant and unimportant to America. And Japan was even farther away. How could they possibly hurt the United States? But the very existence of America was threatened by war as the world got smaller in the 1940's. Tyranny was, it seemed, at the doorstep of the U.S. in that desperate time. And it was a time for unity, courage, sacrifice, and faith. It may have been a bit of an overstatement in thought but Reverend Ferguson did get worked up at times and this morning he was chomping at the bits and ready to deliver. "They'll get their money's worth today," he mumbled to himself as he smiled.

The police department of Denton was not used to serious crimes, at least not the types that plagued other towns and cities. Except for an occasional shoplifter, mail box smasher, or the inevitable Halloween night mischief of toilet papering someone's maple tree, there was virtually no crime. Not that any of the perpetrators would be in church to listen, but maybe the ones in attendance could spread the word like Paul Revere riding along the cobblestone streets of Boston shouting warnings to the good people. "The British are coming," or in modern times, "The evil is coming. Be prepared for it." A widow lady named Judith was heard saying, as she filed into the sanctuary, "Our world has run amok." Many people agreed but they hoped that their town would somehow be spared and Christian ethics would prevail over a world of evil, crime, indulgence, and decadence.

Police chief Sam Phipps sat in his usual chair in his office on that Sunday morning as Deputy Mac Collins made his rounds through town, checking the back streets and looking for anything unusual. It was a quiet morning. "Everything is secure and 10-4," he reported in to headquarters. "It's been a quiet weekend," he added. "I guess everybody's enjoying the nice weather."

The Sunday school crowd was more numerous than usual as each classroom was virtually full. It was a meaningful hour of teaching and learning an important message while finding a relationship between their world, Christianity, and ethics. It was also a time for each age group to commune amongst each other as the teachers strived to find some common message for everyone to take home with them and to apply through the following week.

Finally, after Sunday school was over the faithful churchgoers found their usual places in the sanctuary, reserved by some inalienable right of passage to be in their own personal seat. They entered through the same door every week and exited through the same door when the service was over. They parked in the same parking spot and they hung their hats and coats on the same peg every week.

The Randles took their seats as their two children sat quietly and reverently. The organist, Leona Moffitt, played superbly and with great feeling this morning. Lively she played as people filed in and took their seats. She treated her organ like it was her own. Often seen dusting and polishing it, she really didn't like anyone else using it.

As Reverend James Ferguson started the service, he couldn't help but realize that the Hawkins family was absent, knowing that they were involved with a seriously ill family member at the hospital. He had been called out last night to consult with the Hawkins family, offering some solace and guidance through this difficult time. "Our prayers are with the Hawkins family this morning," he started off. "I'm sure they will back with us next week and things will work out with them."

The church service proceeded as the choir began singing. It was beautiful, just like the flowers and the blue sky outside. Surely the hand of the Lord was touching the congregation for they all felt a surge of energy but, at the same time, were wrapped up in peace and contentment. The choir never sounded so good. Even Edna Matteson, the 90 year old alto, was in perfect pitch. And it was nice to see her in the choir each week. It was wonderful that she was even still with them. But she still sang in the choir and still contributed all she could although her voice was not as strong as it used to be.

Reverend Ferguson inevitably got into his sermon, delivering one of the most dynamic messages of his career. The congregation was mesmerized, to say the least, feeling the power before them. Surely, this sermon was not of human origin but of supernatural powers. Even the preacher was amazed that he could deliver such a sermon. 'I have them in the palm of my hands,' he thought. The floor seemed to shake as his fist hit his large Bible. It seemed to rock the podium, sending cosmic vibrations outward to every person in the sanctuary, who received the messages in their full intended force.

The flock was being transformed from an incongruous hodgepodge of clerks, teachers, construction workers, students, farmers, and the un-employed, to a group of congruent followers of the Christian faith. A family of one. And through this magical medium known as Pastor Ferguson, they were rapt with the power of the Lord, listening to the fire and brimstone sermon with the collective vivacity of a powerful, but caring and energized mob of Christians.

Then suddenly, as Reverend Ferguson paused to catch his breath, a rumble was heard from outside the church. It barely rattled the walls inside but was certainly discernible. 'Maybe a sonic boom,' Phil Hopkins thought. 'A passing thunder cloud,' his wife Jane surmised.But equally puzzling was the sudden drop in brightness outside for just a second. It was as if someone had dimmed the sun for an instant. After all, it was a clear day outside, not a cloud in sight.

Preacher Ferguson continued as he wiped the sweat from his brow with his blue checkered handkerchief and soldiered on. 'I can't lose them now,' he thought. "I have them right where I want them."

"So let the devil walk among us!" he preached in a loud voice. "For we have the power of the Lord to protect us as He shall drive out Satan and cast him into the fiery furnace." He paused, closed his eyes and tilted his head upward as if to look to Heaven. "Walk with us, oh Lord," he shouted. "We're not afraid of you Satan. Get behind us." Leona, caught up in the passion of the moment, accidentally touched one of the organ keys, sending out a rogue note across the length and breadth of the congregation.

"Amen," Tom Morton clearly said from his usual front row seat. Other amens were heard from random locations among the congregation.

The pastor's voice raised another octave as he flung his arms in defiance, "I challenge the devil to come here. We shall cast him out....." Suddenly, the rumbling got more severe. A small piece of plaster dislodged and fell harmlessly from the ceiling, landing exactly in the center of the aisle in the exact center of the sanctuary. The congregation sat frozen in their seats. The fixtures above the crowd began to vibrate and the lights flickered. 'Is this some sort of a sign,' Edna wondered to herself.

"An earth tremor," Mike Randle whispered to his wife Julie. She nodded.

Reverend Ferguson stopped and looked around. For the next five seconds the rumbling continued and then stopped abruptly. The congregation was quiet and a ripple of fear passed its way around the sanctuary and dispersed itself among the crowd. Then the congregation began their own quiet rumblings, passing along their fleeting, analytical thoughts to their neighbor. Then it all got quiet again.

Their pastor then gracefully ended his sermon although he didn't want to. A quick glance at his watch indicated that he was to start winding it up for today. The choir sang the closing hymn, then the prayers, followed by the benediction. It had been a dynamic display of Christian defiance against evil at its demonstrative best. The congregation was energized and ready to face the devil in its purest form. They began filing out of the church as they made brief statements to the minister.

"Bring on Satan," Luke Lycoming said to the preacher as he left the church.

"We're ready for him, aren't we Luke?" Reverend Ferguson agreed, however, by this time he was a bit exhausted from his emotional sermon and only wanted to rest and then have a big Sunday dinner.

The good reverend was greeted by many people as they exited the church. There were many accolades. "It was a great sermon," Jack Hicks said sincerely as his palms sweated and trembled from the onslaught of emotion that emanated from the pulpit. The reverend saw a spark in Jack's eyes that he had not seen since he was baptized twenty years earlier.

Now it was time to go home and enjoy a relaxing day. But something was different as they left the church. The sky was a peculiar color. Not the light blue that it was when they entered the church but a strange shade of light red. The barometer was still high and there was no threat of tornadoes. The sun was suddenly obscured by one small dark and foreboding cloud that seemed to pulsate as it lightened and darkened somewhat, much to the amazement of those who observed it. It was almost like an eclipse. The wind began to blow and there was a slight nip of coolness in the air.

"I think you stirred up something," Hilliard Dukes said to Reverend Ferguson with a nervous smile as he left the church. He had been an usher today and was a faithful member for many years. "I hope I didn't conger up the devil in a literal sense," Ferguson said with a smile. "But I'm beginning to wonder." They both laughed as Hilliard left to check on his elderly mother who lived just down the road. Unfortunately she was unable to attend church anymore but her faithful son always brought her the bulletin.

As Reverend Ferguson and Leona Moffitt left the church, they locked the door behind them, said their goodbyes and started toward their respective cars. Suddenly, from within the church, they could hear the organ playing. It was instantly identified by Leona as Bach's Fugue in G minor. "Must be some kids inside," James said to Leona.

"On second thought," Leona added, "none of those kids could play that. We'd better go back in and see what's going on." Leona didn't like any unauthorized personnel playing her pride and joy. As they entered the church again, there was no one at the organ and, just as suddenly as it started playing, it stopped. "Wow," Leona said with great surprise, "what happened?" The minister just stood there and didn't say anything, but instead looked around for clues.

Meanwhile, the Randles entered their house to discover their dog Rufus a bit agitated. He was restless and was growling under his breath. "I wonder what's bothering him?" Julie asked. "I assume he's a bit aggravated at the earth tremors we've just had," Mike responded. "Dogs have a sixth sense about those things."

"Maybe he's heard rumbling underground," Janet added. "Dogs can hear things we can't."

"I'm not so sure that was really an earthquake," Mike observed as he scratched his head. Maybe some military thing."

"You're giving me the willies," Julie added as she headed toward the kitchen to get the pot roast started.

Meanwhile back at the church, James and Leona were still trying to figure out what going on with the organ. They finally decided it must have been a short in the electrical system, something that needed fixing as soon as possible. Maybe it wasn't Bach after all. Maybe it was just some random notes that were produced by a malfunctioning organ. But as they left the church again and locked the door, it happened again. The organ started playing, not as before but extremely loud, almost like an explosion. In fact, it increased to the point that the auditory concussion broke out two windows in the church sanctuary. Glass shattered and spewed into the parking lot. The minister's car was showered with pieces of stained glass. Leona's car was untouched. Then, the music stopped.

Hilliard Dukes ran from his mother's house to see what had happened."What blew up?" he asked in a panic. The stunned Reverend James and Leona stood in total confusion. "I wish I knew," he responded.

Jack Hicks also returned to inquire. "I heard something from down the street and wondered what was going on."

Back on Wick Street, two blocks away, the Randles heard the noise and ran outside. "It came from the church," Martin said to his family.

They all four hustled down the street to the church as others were beginning to gather, including Chief Phipps and Deputy Collins.

"What the heck happened?" Chief Phipps asked, almost out of breath.

"I wish I knew," the pastor said again as he explained the strange occurrence.

They all went inside to survey the damage and fortunately only the two windows were blown out. No other damage was observed. No evidence of an explosive device was found and the organ was still in one piece and operable. There was no trace of smoke or any strange odors.

"This is really bizarre," Mike Randle told the sheriff. Outside, the sky was still a strange shade of light red and the dark cloud still blocked out the sun, refusing to move. The crowd of people, including Hilliard Dukes, the Randles, James Ferguson, Leona Moffitt, Jack Hicks, and others, turned their attention to the church cemetery, adjacent to the church. A beam of light was suddenly shining down on the grave site of Marvin Maxwell, who had been buried twenty years ago to the day. The beam was red like a laser.

The preacher looked up at the sky, noticing the beam of light was making its way through a tiny crack in the dark cloud that hid the sun. Marvin was an old miserly loner that was known as a rich old curmudgeon. He didn't like people and the people didn't like him. Before he died, he took out all his money and valuables from the bank, which amounted to a considerable sum, and hid them somewhere that was never found. On his deathbed, he vowed that he would take his fortune with him. That was the last thing he ever said. He died a lonely, bitter old man of 85 years and was buried in the church cemetery in a private service, privy only to a few close relatives. People said that the only reason he was buried in the church cemetery was because it was free.

"He was an evil and selfish old man," Leona stated. "He's probably causing all this commotion."

Just then, a bolt of lightning struck the ground just yards from the group standing in front of the church. A bright flash followed by an ear shattering explosion. Chief Phipps called in to headquarters. Other reports of natural disturbances were coming in.

"Do you see that strange cloud covering the sun?" he asked the dispatcher.

"Yes," she responded. "We've been getting flooded with calls from all over town. Reports of mysterious noises and flashes of light. Also, sporadic power outages and television interference."

"Just in the Denton area?" Phipps asked.

"10-4, Chief. It seems to be confined to Denton but most of the reports are from close to the church."

"I don't know what to do," Chief Phipps said to Pastor Ferguson.

"I've never seen anything like it," the minister answered. "I'm almost beginning to think I had something to do with it with my sermon."

"I don't see how that could be,:" Mrs. Randle answered. Suddenly, two boys, Jeff and Tom Hawkins, came running to the scene.

"Anything we can do to help?" Jeff asked.

"Nothing at the moment," the minister said. "But nice of you to ask. Do you have any idea what could be causing this?" The boys were in a quandary like everyone else. The cloud continued to block out the sun except for one solitary red beam of light that bore down on Mr. Maxwell's grave site.

For all that had happened, things were getting worse. Strange noises were heard. The ground shook and an eerie sense of foreboding was felt by many who lived near the church. Some people even considered getting in their cars and leaving town until things calmed down.

After much deliberation, the minister thought of something. "That strange light," he told Chief Phipps and Deputy Collins. "It still is shining down of Maxwell's grave stone. It's like a pointer. Do you suppose it's trying to tell us something?"

"I'll believe anything now," the chief said.

"You may be onto something, pastor," Mike Randle stated. "Whatever is happening may be coming from that grave."

"That's crazy," Leona said. "That's like some evil spirit or something."

Bolts of lightning were still striking as if they were under attack by some unknown force.

"I think we should call in the army or something," Deputy Collins stated.

"I have a better idea," the minister said calmly. "Let's dig up Maxwell's grave. That light is pointing to it. I think it's trying to tell us something."

"I think we better leave well enough alone," Hilliard answered. "Maybe this will blow over soon." Then, as soon as Hilliard spoke his mind, a bolt of lightning hit the church steeple and it exploded, sending splinters of wood raining down on everyone. Fortunately, no one was hurt as it scattered all over the parking lot and onto the churchyard. "On the other hand....." Hilliard added with a controlled air of panic in his voice. "We need to do something."

Chief Phipps was stunned. But, however, at this point, his town was on the verge of mass panic. He was willing to try anything. "Ok, everyone with shovels, go get them. We're digging up that grave."

The church custodian, Fred Schultz was the first to start digging, followed by Jack Hicks, then Mike Randle and his kids. Everyone with a shovel or a strong back was drafted as they feverishly dug deeper and deeper. Through the red clay dirt they went as the strange red light continued to shine down, pointing the way to Maxwell's permanent eternal resting place. Winds continued to howl and the lightning continued to strike. The birds had even disappeared as if a giant serpent was lurking about. It was like a scene out of a horror movie, the towns people acting as one, pitting themselves against invisible forces of evil, trying what they could to stifle it.

At last they struck something hard. "We found it," Phil Hopkins shouted as his shovel rang out with sparks flying. It produced a sharp metallic sound, like the distant peel of a church bell. He had hit the big silver cast iron vault. Inside the vault was the casket of Marvin Maxwell. They had planned to open up the vault if necessary as well as the casket.

"Now what do we do?" Leona said as she grabbed a shovel and joined the men.

"Keep digging," the minister instructed. As they dug deeper, they hit something soft. Plastic bags had been buried around and under the iron vault. The grave diggers began retrieving them and tossed them up to Reverend Ferguson and the police chief.

As they opened them, they discovered money and jewels, gold and silver. The better part of the afternoon was spent retrieving the fortune that Maxwell had somehow managed to leave behind intact in numerous bags.

They piled up the booty in the fellowship hall as it got larger and larger. A committee was formed on the spot to count the money which now was in excess of a million dollars. The jewels and gold were a different story and it would have to be assayed by a professional. "I believe this belongs to the church," Pastor Ferguson said as he looked at it. "I'm no lawyer," Deputy Collins stated as he guarded it, "but I'd say since it was not in the casket and was on church property, it would belong to the church."

When the last bag was brought to the surface, the winds increased and the sky darkened. More vicious bolts of angry lightning hit dangerously close to the spectators as they ran for cover. The church shook violently as shingles flew off the roof and more windows shattered. The organ played again until smoke began to rise from it and it quit, presumably from the stresses. "My beautiful organ is ruined," Leona said with a tear in her eye. She put her arms around it as if to console a sick relative.

With everyone now out of the hole and having moved away from the grave, Reverend Ferguson bravely stood alone over it. Violent winds whipped his hair into a tangled mass. His tie flung wildly around his neck and his eyes squinted from the dust and sand churned up. He suddenly tore off the beautiful stainless steel cross from around his neck and tossed it into the grave.

He kneeled down on the edge of the grave and said a few words in prayer, known only to himself and never divulged to anyone else. For what seemed like hours but were only a few minutes, he stayed there frozen in prayer.

Then suddenly and mercifully, the red beam of light disappeared. The solitary black cloud that was obscuring the sun vanished. The winds died down and all was calm and bright again. The birds began to sing and flew back to the trees. And the sky returned to a beautiful shade of light blue.

Reverend Ferguson rose from his feet as the crowd began to move closer, ever so cautiously. He instructed the men to cover up the grave again, leaving his cross on top of the steel vault to be buried too.

"Folks," he said, "we've witnessed something frightening and supernatural today. We, or rather I, unleashed Satan, somehow. The embodiment of evil rested in that grave. Burying money and valuables with malice in a church cemetery planted the seeds of evil. Somehow, in my sermon today, I managed to cause those seeds to germinate."

"It's all over now," Mike Randle said as sweat dripped from his brow.

"I sure hope it is," the reverend stated.

"What did you say in prayer over the grave?" Leona asked reverently.

"I can't divulge that prayer," the reverend said. "It's reserved for the most evil and vile circumstances."

"Amen to that," Phil Hopkins said as he threw down his shovel and dusted himself off. "I've had enough excitement for one afternoon."

Many months passed since that day. The fortune that was left behind was determined to be legal property of the church. It was used for repairs and a multitude of other things that the church and community needed badly. Leona Moffitt got a new organ, larger and more beautiful than the one before. And through it all, a curse became a blessing, thanks to a preacher whose fire and brimstone sermon touched not only the congregation but the dark evil world buried beyond the grave. Reverend James Ferguson would never again raise the devil.

# Chapter 5

# A Visit To Skytropolis

*I*t was a warm June night, just outside the small town of Fairmont, Illinois. Around two A.M. Mary Caroline and her younger sister Elizabeth slept, glad that summer time was finally here. And they dreamed of summer camp, swimming trips, visits to Chicago and to Joliet to see their cousins, and a multitude of other things that kids love to do while they bask in the joys of being free in the summer, between school terms. However, on this particular night, while the town and areas around Fairmont slept peacefully, something was astir in the sky above them. It was something strange, to be sure, at least from an Earthling's perspective, and the silver object slowly and silently descended through the warm summer haze in the wee hours of this particular morning as it gradually got closer to the clover covered field below their house.

As it came closer to the ground, the cows stirred only slightly, shook their heads and went back to their late night snacking, occasionally looking up but not being concerned enough to be scared. The ship made no sound but quietly and stealthily descended upon this quiet rural sleeping community. The good citizens of Fairmont were totally unaware of its presence.

Mary Caroline stirred as she turned in her bed, briefly opening her eyes and catching a glimpse of something that was approaching, possibly a brief flash of light from the moon's reflection of the strange descending craft. At first, she didn't think anything about it but then awoke with a start and glanced out the window. "Oh my," she said quietly to herself, being careful not to wake Elizabeth in the bed on the other side of the room. "What in the world could that be?" she said to herself as she rubbed her eyes.

She rose from her bed and opened the window. By now the mysterious craft was settling quietly on the grass about three hundred yards from their house. It appeared to be about fifty feet long and about twenty feet high. It still didn't make a sound but she could see it clearly as the moon reflected silver white light toward her window. There were strange blue lights on the side. She looked over at Elizabeth, who was sound asleep. "Elizabeth," she said quietly as not to wake up their parents in the bedroom down the hall. Elizabeth opened her eyes and looked up at her sister.

"What is it?" she asked as she yawned. "Time to get up?"

"You gotta see this," Mary Caroline said as she pointed down toward the field. "I think it's a spaceship or something."

Elizabeth jumped out of bed and ran to the window. "Wow!" she said with as much excitement as she could muster at two o'clock in the morning. "Maybe we'd better tell Mom and Dad."

"No," Mary Caroline said. "I want to go down there and get a closer look. If Mom and Dad know about this they won't let us go."

"Us?" Elizabeth said with caution. "I'm not sure I want to get any closer than here."

"It's just sitting there, not hurting anything," Mary Caroline reasoned. She replaced her pajamas with a shirt and pants and put on her shoes.

"Well," Elizabeth stated, "maybe we *could* go down and have just a peek at a safe distance, then we'll come back home. Right?"

"It's a deal," her sister agreed. Elizabeth clumsily put on her clothes and shoes as best she could, coming out of a deep sleep. "I was dreaming about a trip to the beach," she added, "not a UFO."

The two curious sisters made their way carefully out the window and onto the ground below, being careful not to step on Mom's flower bed. The neighborhood was quiet as the two girls walked slowly and cautiously down the hill and toward the silver object that had come quietly out of the sky and plopped itself in the field of clover.

As they got closer, the strange object sparkled from the moonlight. It was producing a soft humming sound and the whole area around it glowed a bluish white as if illuminated by some invisible light.

"Don't be afraid, kids," a voice suddenly said as if it came from nowhere. "I'm Sharkey LeGrand from Skytropolis."

They turned around with a start and saw a tall man standing behind them dressed in a metallic green suit. He looked like a normal human being, not like a little green man with large eyes like they expected. His voice was calm and soothing and the girls felt they had nothing to be afraid of, at least at the moment. They followed him to the craft that landed in the field but kept a safe distance.

They moved closer with Elizabeth being careful to stay safely behind her sister. Soon, they got a good close up view of the ship. It was sleek and white in color. It had a red stripe running along the side from front to back. As the stripe went aft, it flared into three more stripes toward a vertical tail fin. Three soft blue running lights were arranged in a straight line just below the red stripe on each side of the ship. The nose was sharply pointed and there were vents underneath. The windows were glazed with a type of bright silver substance. A green fire-breathing dragon creature was painted on both sides of the tail fin. A name in strange writing was painted in black letters toward the front end of the ship under the cockpit area. Six gold stars were painted below the name. Two tail vent pipes were painted flat black and were near the underside of the ship.

A hatch opened as Sharkey entered the ship he called the *Dragon*. He turned around and said, "Come on in, kids. It's okay; you can meet the rest of the crew."

Mary Caroline looked at Elizabeth as if to seek approval from each other. "Do you think we should?" Elizabeth asked. "Let's just peek inside."

"Well," Mary Caroline stated with confidence, "nobody has hurt us so far. I really don't think they mean us any harm."

They entered the magnificent ship. Inside, they saw a myriad of lights, gauges, dials, switches, and strange looking objects. They could clearly see Sharkey now, along with his three surprised crew members as they turned about from their duties and looked at the two night travelers.

Amazingly, Mary Caroline noticed, they all looked like humans from Earth. They spoke English and seemed very polite. They were all dressed in the same green metallic type suits. Sharkey explained that they had learned their earth language and could speak it very well so they had no problem communicating.

Sharkey then introduced the members of his crew. "This is Wilma Lurking, our weapons specialist, Bobo Whalebone, the pilot and Stretch McGirt, the navigator."

"Hello there," Bobo said with a wave and a friendly smile as he turned around.

"Greetings and welcome to our ship," Stretch stated as he also produced a charming smile.

"What beautiful children," Wilma said as she rose from her seat and walked over to Mary Caroline and Elizabeth, kneeling in front of them.

The children felt an immediate bond with Wilma. Her dark eyes contrasted beautifully against her medium length hair. She was wearing a strange pair of earrings made from some kind of un-earthly metal that glistened, changing colors in the light. "These earrings are made from magnetanium, a valuable mineral not found on your planet," she explained after noticing they were admiring them. It would be considered priceless since it would be the only one of its kind. It's the hardest substance known in the universe."

"What are you doing out this time of night?" Sharkey asked the girls.

"We saw your ship and decided to investigate," Elizabeth said.

"Why did you land on Earth?" Mary Caroline asked as she looked around the ship.

"We came to replenish our nitrogen supply," Stretch said. "We'll only be here a few minutes."

"What do you need nitrogen for?" Elizabeth inquired.

"I'll let Sharkey explain it," Stretch stated.

Sharkey then spoke, "We need it for our rocket engine," he explained. "Our TXQ-35A rocket motor relies on nitrogen and an element called 'lithurium,'

which you don't have here on Earth either. Nitrogen is so abundant in your atmosphere that we come here periodically."

"Wow!" Elizabeth said with awe. "How do you find your way around the galaxy?"

"I'll let our navigator, Stretch, explain that," Sharkey said.

"It's rather simple," Stretch said as he took the children to his station. They looked at a myriad of lights, screens, and switches. "Here's how we find our way around the galaxies. Every major object in the known universe has a navigational number attached to it. This includes planets, stars, and nebula. Earth's designation is 163-3-0016-0138-2163. Each number represents a part of the universal designation. When we input this into our NavTrek3000 computer, the ship automatically heads for that location. Of course we monitor the course and can override it manually if we want to. Bobo can show you how he pilots the ship."

The kids then walked over to Bobo's station where he was more than glad to show them how he flies the Dragon. Bobo was friendly and had a kind voice.

"Although the Dragon can virtually fly itself, as Stretch explained, we still have to be able to maneuver it in and out of planets. Also, if we are under attack, we can do things a computer can't do."

"At least he likes to think he can," Sharkey said with a smile from across the room.

Bobo smirked and continued. "Sharkey's just jealous because he's not as good a pilot as I am. Anyway, if something were to happen to the computer, I would be able to fly the ship to wherever we're going."

"What kind of weapons do you have," Mary Caroline asked Sharkey as she looked at Wilma's sidearm.

"This is Wilma's specialty," Sharkey stated. "She can explain all that to you."

"We have the most powerful weapon in the galaxy," Wilma explained. It's called the 'Riptron II.' It can target fourteen separate objects simultaneously. It has a disintegrator-regenerator that can break down a target's atomic structure and re-assemble it at a different location. It also has a feature called 'freeze frame' that can cause an object to stop moving immediately.

"That's incredible," Elizabeth said. "But what's that weapon you have on your belt?"

Wilma took out her side arm and explained. "It's a BM-88B, or Blast Master 88, model B, hand held weapon. It has a variety of features including single beam and scatter blast with radar tracking, personal force field, and sky block, all with a range of over 2,000 yards. Would you like to see it in action?"

The girls both said yes enthusiastically.

They stepped outside the ship as Wilma aimed it toward a large bolder. She pulled the trigger as a blue stream of light shot from the gun and immediately disintegrated the rock into dust. "Wow," Mary Caroline said with awe. "I'm glad you're our friend. At least I hope you are."

"I'm definitely your friend," Wilma said with a warm smile.

"Dad's wanted to get rid of that rock for a long time, anyway," Elizabeth explained.

Sharkey stuck his head of out the hatch, "We're getting ready to take off now. You kids better get back up to your house now."

"Can you take us for a ride in your ship?" the children begged.

"Sorry," Sharkey said with remorse. "It's against regulations. Not that we wouldn't want to, it's just that we aren't allowed."

The kids looked terribly disappointed. "Ah, can't we take them for a little spin around Earth?" Wilma asked as she winked at the children.

"Well, I guess we could take them for a short ride," Sharkey said.

Wilma escorted them back into the *Dragon* and she closed the hatch.

"I don't think a little ride would hurt anything," Bobo said as he started flipping switches. Strange noises were heard as a small amount of vibration rumbled through the ship. The girl's ears popped slightly from the pressurization of the cabin.

Soon, the powerful starship called the *Dragon* lifted off from the field as they began their ascent through the wee hours of the morning. The town of Fairmont continued to sleep peacefully as the silver ship picked up speed. Mary Caroline and Elizabeth had a great view as they watched their town below them get smaller. The streetlights got dimmer the higher they got.

In just a few seconds they reached a height of a hundred miles and then they accelerated on an angle and were high above earth, passing over oceans and deserts. The children could see an ice cap on the North Pole and the stars were clearer and brighter than they had ever seen.

"You're a great pilot, Bobo," Mary Caroline said as she continued to look out the window.

"Piece of cake," Bobo stated as he looked pleased at their approval.

After a few minutes, Sharkey gave the order to return to Earth so they could safely deposit their two passengers when Elizabeth asked, "Where exactly are you all from?"

"Like Sharkey said, we're from Skytropolis," Wilma said as she sat close to the two girls. "It's a man-made world that was built many years ago. It's pretty much like a normal planet with all the things you have here on Earth but much more. It revolves around a star just like your earth revolves around the sun. Skytropolis, along with the city of the same name, is a beautiful place to live. There's another large city on the opposite side of the planet called Astronia. They counter balance each other."

"Where is it?" the children asked.

"It's about a hundred light years from Earth," Sharkey interjected.

"How long does it take you to get there?"

"About ten minutes," Stretch said, "unless we get lost or if the NavTrek 3000 malfunctions."

"That's impossible," Mary Caroline said. "You can't go that fast."

"We obviously can exceed the speed of light many times over," Sharkey explained.

"Can we see Skytropolis," the two girls asked respectfully. If it only takes a few minutes, why not take us there for a look?"

"Oh, why not," Sharkey said. "We've already broken the rule for transporting unauthorized personnel. What can they do to us?"

The rest of the crew cheered, for they had already grown fond of the two late night space travelers.

"Away we go," Bobo stated as he poured on the coal.

Soon, the Earth was a shrinking speck in the window. In a few seconds, it completely disappeared as they sped through the dark void of outer space. Stars looked like streaks of bending light as they peered out the window.

In just a few minutes, Stretch announced, "Approaching Skytropolis," and they began decelerating.

Out the window, Mary Caroline and Elizabeth could see a tiny speck getting brighter. It shimmered like a diamond. As they approached they could see what appeared to be a huge city with many colored lights. They could see mountains and forests in the distance. It was early evening there as darkness had begun to fall on Skytropolis. Bright lights from the city, however, made it look almost like daytime.

"We're coming in for a landing," Bobo announced as Wilma reached over and pulled the two girls close.

"Skytropolis is protected by a large transparent canopy," Sharkey explained. "We enter through an opening very high up."

"You're really going to enjoy this," Wilma said.

As the *Dragon* landed softly on the pad, the girls looked out the window. Never in their life had they seen anything so spectacular and beautiful. Different colored lights as far as the eye could see with strange looking vehicles moving in all directions, traveled on a cushion of air with no wheels. Skyscrapers towered into the sky so high that you could barely see the top. A clear canopy covered the entire manmade planet. The stars were so plentiful and dense, they looked like solid streaks across the sky, and each star with, perhaps, their own earth-like worlds. There seemed to be millions or even billions of them as far as you could see and beyond into the vast eternal endlessness of the universe. .

As they peered out the window of the *Dragon,* the people on Skytropolis looked like humans on Earth and, as Sharkey explained, they were all from the same galaxy and made up of the same elements and were, therefore, very similar in appearance and biological structure as Earthlings.

Bobo shut off the engines and opened the hatch. Waiting there was their boss and friend, Inspector Archibald Locknose, head of the Space Patrol. Sharkey was the first to come out, followed by Bobo and Stretch. "Where's Wilma?" the inspector asked as he peered inside the hatch.

Suddenly, she emerged with the two young girls, one on each side, holding their hands. The stunned inspector just stood there in disbelief, but was immediately charmed by the two smiling children who walked over to him.

"Hello sir," they said politely as they shook his hand.

Locknose nodded.

"I thought there was a rule about such things," Locknose stated to Sharkey. "I hope you have a good explanation for this."

"Well," Sharkey explained, "we thought you might like to adopt a couple of children."

"Why would I do that," Locknose answered, "I have four working for me already."

'Good one," Bobo retorted with a hearty laugh.

"I see you've been keeping bad company with Sharkey and the Space Pirates," the inspector said to the kids.

"Wow," Elizabeth said. "Are you really pirates?"

"Used to be," Sharkey explained. "We're working for the Space Patrol now."

They also introduced the children to Matt Starr, Space Detective, trained in part by Sharkey and his crew and assigned to inter-galactic investigations of criminal activities.

They all went inside the inspector's office as Sharkey explained how the kids happened to be on the ship. Locknose couldn't get upset with Sharkey too much because they'd been through a lot together. Besides, Sharkey and his crew brought a lot of space criminals to justice and were heroes in Skytropolis, not to mention many other planets. The kids did not know, but each of the six stars painted on the *Dragon* represented enemy space ships that were destroyed in combat.

"Just don't let this happen again," the inspector said to Sharkey and his crew.

"I hope we didn't get Sharkey and his crew in trouble," Mary Caroline said as she looked up at the inspector.

"No, of course not," he answered kindly as he looked at the kids. "Don't worry about it."

By now, the two kids were totally awed by all that was around them and the inspector agreed to let Sharkey and his crew take them on a tour of the city, as long as they got them back home on Earth before morning.

So off they went into the wondrous city of Skytropolis, a manmade world with an endless number of things to explore. Unfortunately, they had only a short time to look and experience this world among the stars. Inspector Locknose provided a car called a *Star Streak AU 3.26* and a driver named Lieutenant Lex, who was Locknose's chief assistant. Sharkey and his crew called him "Lexey." They all piled into the spacious back seat area of the limousine-type vehicle, It had an open top so the children could take in all the wonders of Skytropolis.

They cruised down Alpha Boulevard, a wide avenue that seemed to go for miles. Here, vehicles were moving in both directions, and office buildings lined the street where people were working late. There were restaurants, grocery stores, night clubs, houses and apartments, churches, and hotels. Many people were walking along the sidewalks going in and out of stores. Outside the city were vast farms with country steams, forests, and mountains. Trucks would carry food to the city from the farms.

For a few moments, Mary Caroline and Elizabeth thought they were back on Earth. Lexey stopped the car at a traffic light and the children looked up. They saw buildings so high they could not see the tops. Above the buildings was the clear canopy that protected Skytropolis. As they looked through it, they were rapt by the full magnificence of the Milky Way Galaxy, for they were still home in a much broader sense than they could fully appreciate or comprehend. Stars sparkled with such brilliance and density that they looked like solid silvery-white ribbons, swirling in spiral shapes as they trailed off and dispersed into the heavens, taking with them millions more stars with other worlds beyond. These stars sparkled like diamonds above them and glistened like a heavenly halo.

Finally, they moved down Aurora Street and they passed the Stratosphere Night Club where various performers were known to have jump-started their careers into inter-galactic stardom. They passed Mo and Danny Boy's Crab House. They passed the Equinox Arena where many important sporting events took place. Big star wrestlers and boxers like Tiger Lyon, Bulldog Mongrel, Runaway Trane, Choir Boy Crusher, and Rogue Mangler, were scheduled to duke it out for a big payoff. They kept driving until Sharkey finally spoke.

"Stop here," Sharkey said to Lexey. It was the Carnivalis Spectacularis,

"I think the kids will really enjoy this," Wilma said excitedly.

They got out of the car and walked into the carnival area. The sights, sounds, and smells were not that different from a carnival on earth. They stopped at a concession stand and Stretch bought the children some Polaris Popcorn.

"This is one of my favorite treats," Wilma stated as she held their hands tightly so they wouldn't get separated in the crowd. Mary Caroline and Elizabeth thought the popcorn was the best treat they had ever tasted.

"We don't have a lot of time," Sharkey explained, "so we're going to see a few things we think you'll enjoy."

They played *Spontaneous Mutaneous*, a video game where you can mastermind the creation of all sorts of mutants using different types of DNA.

Then they watched as they evolved into various odd looking creatures.

They got to ride the Hungry Dragon, in which the participants sat on a giant plate in front of a simulated dragon's mouth. The plate would vibrate as its riders struggled to stay upright. As the plate vibrated, it also tilted toward the dragon's mouth which opened, sending the children down its throat as it 'swallowed' the hapless customers. They slid down to an opening behind the dragon where the people exited, tumbling onto a large pillow, unhurt, amused, and exhilarated.

By far, however, the ride they enjoyed the most was the *Regenerator Reducer*. The paying customers were placed in a tube where their molecules were disassembled, only to reappear in the same form only two inches high in a tiny town complete with toy train, cars, doll houses, and other small objects. The kids could ride, play, and explore for ten minutes, at which time they had to return to their normal size.

But sooner than anyone wanted, it came time to leave the carnival and head back to Space Patrol headquarters. Their two hours were up and they had seen only a fraction of the wonderful attractions. They took a different route down Stardust Boulevard where they passed the Cosmo Drome, a large outdoor complex for concerts, sporting events, and conventions. It's where they held the *Field Of Stars Festival*. A concert was going on and they could hear music in the distance, echoing eerily through the parking lot. By now Mary Caroline and Elizabeth were getting tired and sleepy and it was about time to go leave.

Soon, however, they were back at Space Patrol headquarters where Inspector Locknose was waiting for them. "Take them back to Earth," the Inspector said as they exited the car.

"It's about time to go home, kids," Wilma whispered to them.

"No," Elizabeth said. "We want to stay a little longer." Mary Caroline nodded in agreement.

Sharkey and his crew immediately boarded the *Dragon* with the two children with them. Inspector Locknose was sorry to see them go although he knew it was for the best that they return to their home planet.

"It's been fun," the inspector said to Sharkey, "but don't do this again."

"Thanks, Inspector," Sharkey said with a smile.

"Crank it up, Bobo," Sharkey ordered as the crew took their places. The girls sleepily looked out the window as the *Dragon* lifted off the pad smoothly and soared into the sky and through the opening in Skytropolis' canopy. As they sped away, the girls looked back and saw their wonderful magical world glisten in the night sky as it gradually got dimmer until finally it disappeared. In a few minutes Earth started coming into view. Soon, they could see the blue and white sphere getting larger.

As they approached the clover field just outside of Fairmont, Illinois, Wilma handed the girls something. "Here's a little gift to remember us by," she said. Wilma took off her earrings and gave each of them one. "Remember me telling you it was made of magnetanium? It's very valuable and your scientists won't be able to identify it or use it. So they are priceless and indestructible, like our friendship."

"Thank you," the girls said in unison as they hugged Wilma. Soon, Mary Caroline and Elizabeth had their feet on the solid ground of the good Earth. They could hear crickets chirping and felt the cool moist early morning air. The sky was getting brighter in the east and they said their goodbyes.

"We had a wonderful time," Mary Caroline said as she and Elizabeth took turns hugging the rest of the crew.

"The pleasure was all ours," Sharkey answered with a smile. "Now get back to your house before your parents start looking for you."

They climbed back up the hill and into their bedroom. They watched as the *Dragon* silently climbed into the early morning sky until it finally disappeared.

"I don't think we should tell anyone about this," Elizabeth said.

"They wouldn't believe it anyway," Mary Caroline answered.

# Chapter 6

# It's Only Money

*I*f I have more than I need, I'm rich," Herbert Godfrey used to say in his lean years of poverty. He somehow rose from the depths of desperation and dearth and vaulted up the ladder of success to become a self-made millionaire. It was quite a feat, to be sure, as he clobbered the opposition in a legal way to rise to the top rung of the ladder. Long past were the days when he worked in the local hardware store as a teenager during summers to make extra money and bagged groceries on weekends during the school year.

And now it was time to enjoy the fruits of his labor. He lived in a mansion on Snob Hill and drove several expensive cars. He wore Italian silk suits and was shod in alligator shoes. Diamond rings were on several fingers and a solid gold chain hung around his neck, hidden by his shirt and tie. He was literally in the lap of luxury and to make things even better, the money was still pouring in. Long past was the time he 'needed' anything. It was now just gravy on the steak and icing on the cake. In fact, he dined on lobster for lunch or anything else he desired, perfect for excursions on his yacht or flights in his private jet. What could be better?

It all started in his hometown, the name is not important. We'll call it Podunk or Backwater or even Boondocks. It was a nice little town but the opportunities for an aspiring business man were limited to owning a small store or working at a gas station. People would sit on the porch and count cars as they went by. They hoed weeds in their garden and canned vegetables. They picked apples off the ground and made them into applesauce, and along with peaches and other fruits, froze them for a cold winter day treat.

The people of this little community had cellars of canned tomatoes and beans along with homemade soup. They cut wood for their fireplaces to save money on heating bills. They worked at low paying jobs but were glad to have a steady paycheck. They went to church and trusted in God to help provide them with the necessities of life. They had all they needed, at least they thought. Herb had other ideas.

He was bored with this life and wanted something more. In his youth, he was just average. He was not anti-social but preferred to be alone and read. And he read and he read and the more he read the more he realized there was much more to life than being a small fish in a small pond. He went to college and studied business. And somewhere along the way, he lost the roots of his past but gained a spark of enthusiasm for a fulfilled life of material things. It was off the big city and the land of opportunities for Herbert Godfrey.

Then one night during a midsummer night's slumber, he had a dream. Not just an ordinary dream but one of those graphic ones you have just before you wake up. He dreamed about an invention, or rather an idea for something bigger than anything he had ever dreamed of in the conscious state. It would make him famous and rich beyond his wildest imagination. He couldn't wait to get up and write it down. And as the mockingbird blared outside his window with a hundred different songs, Herbert's head was filled with a hundred ways to exploit his brainstorm.

"Comfort stations," he murmured to himself. "Or maybe I'll call it 'comfort houses.'" He called the board of directors for an emergency meeting at his office. In an hour, they were all seated in their places around an oblong table for the revelation of a lifetime.

Herb took the pointer and his rapidly prepared set of drawings and began speaking. "Here's the idea. We'll build small single story, four room houses all around the country, preferably beside highways. They will have water, a wood heater with firewood, and a toilet. Nothing more except an attendant who checks on things once in a while.  Anyone who wants to spend the night there or just hang out and rest can do so for free, however, we will have a donation box for the users to show their appreciation."

The room was silent. "Well, what do you think?" Herb spurted, looking for some support.

"Well," Marvin Pell said in a quiet voice. "Don't we have rest stops along the highways?  Isn't that the same thing?"

"You can't spend the night there," Herb explained. "Besides, you can't loiter either. There's no intimacy at a rest stop and no privacy."

"And no fireplace," Betsy Shorts stated. "I really like fireplaces."

"Hmmm," Pete Wilkins said with a nod. "I'm beginning to see what you mean. It might work. But what kind of people would be staying here besides the homeless or maybe transients with nowhere else to stay for the night."

"And who's to say they wouldn't try to just move in a stay forever with their ten kids?" Alex Taggett added.

"There would be certain rules," Herb said. "Maybe a limit to the number of days and maybe even restricting it to adults."

"I sort of like the idea," Herman Brinks said with a smile. "I can picture these dotted all around the highways and not just the interstates, a lot of the side roads too."

"Maybe one in every town," Jay Botz added.

And so, the idea that Herbert Godfrey hatched out in a dream came to fruition. The board certainly had the money to get it going and before long, Herb's 'Comfort Stations' were the sensation of the country. He even built 'Comfort Boxes' in crowded cities that were one room houses where people could stay and have a certain amount of privacy, especially if all the hotels were full. A lot of friendships were made at these locations; graffiti filled the walls with people's names and the dates they stayed. An attendant kept law and order and the temporary residents managed to keep the places relatively clean. Donations were pouring in from all over the country. It was a gold mine and a juggernaut of financial success with no indication of slowing down.

But with everything man made, it did slow down. Then one day, things began to go wrong. Herb wasn't sure exactly how it started. How could something so perfect go wrong? Like a well tuned racing engine, something broke inside and if it wasn't fixed, it would be a smoldering pile of useless junk.

Lawsuits, regulations, over extending, and a multitude of other complications began, not to mention bad investments and corruption within the system. His profits began to dwindle. Banks foreclosed on some of his investments and the stock market began going sour. It was bad times ahead for Herb and he began to actually lose money, something he hadn't done in many years. Then, he overcompensated for his losses and made some bad investments. But he still had a fortune - several million dollars of liquid assets. But the Herb Godfrey empire was in trouble, especially when he was forced to sell his mansion.

He decided that the banks were no place for his money so he built a large building on some of his property. It would be safe there and he could watch it.

Then he had to hire guards to protect the money and security systems. More money was spent on re-enforced steel walls with razor wire and a couple of guard towers. 'No interest on the money,' he though to himself but at least it is safe from embezzlers and crooked bank presidents. 'Let the rest of my empire crumble to dust, At least I have my money.'

His beloved Comfort Stations began to close from lack of funds to pay the attendants. And to make matters worse, government rules and regulations were choking the freedom that was so necessary for his project to succeed. "Improper restroom facilities," they said. "Dangerous wood burning fireplaces, not enough security." And the list went on and on. And lawsuits from people who claimed injuries in his little bungalows were beginning to pour in. His legal expenses were enormous.

"Settle out of court !!" That was the solution. He didn't need bad publicity.

"They're ruining me," he said to one of his guards as he spoke of the government regulations, criminals, scam artists, and others hoping to make a fast settlement buck. "I just won't allow it."

Beefing up security around his Fort Knox style building was even more expense. Rumor was that the new airport would direct traffic right over his building. "Must get radar to warn us of a possible remote control airplane that could be loaded with explosives," he told the guards. "We might even put in guided missiles to shoot them down before they get here."

This was the last straw. The guards were beginning to worry about his mental state. Besides, money was flying out of the building faster than it was coming in. Soon, you could hear your echo as you wandered around the cargo holds. His family was forced to seek help for Herb, checking out the gray matter from the neck up seemed like the logical thing to do.

While all this was going on, his beloved company went belly up. Convincing the doctors he was still within control of his senses worked, however, and he was back on the job. But what job? Problem was, his building was virtually empty now. The guards quit and he was forced to sell what few assets he had left to get out from under.

He was now broke and forced to return to his childhood home. The old home place was still there and fortunately his family, who now controlled it, let him live there. It was back to the roots of his youth.

No more fancy cars or airplanes or jets. He was just another one of the residents who found a job working in the hardware store. He bagged groceries on weekends. He finally found what he was really looking for but he'd been around the world to find it.

"If I have more than I need, I'm rich," he mumbled to himself with a smile as he filled Mrs. Peabody's bag in the check out line at the grocery store.

# Chapter 7

# Welcome to Oakville

John and Doris Resnick drove happily down highway six as they plied their way toward Grantsburg to visit poor ailing Aunt Louise. She was a bit of a hypochondriac but nonetheless, a dear sweet soul, full of generosity, especially when it came to the dinner table. She also seemed to know everything going on around her, keeping her eyes open and her ears to the ground. In her advancing years, she seemed to be in touch even more, falling back on her years of wisdom and knowledge.

John and Doris were about fifty miles from their destination when John decided to make a slight navigational change that would delay their arrival by some thirty minutes.

"Are you sure?" Doris spouted, sounding a bit fatigued. "We've been driving for hours. I'd kind of like to get there."

"But we've never been on Route forty," John responded. "They say it's a really pretty drive in the country. Besides, it will only add a short time to our trip."

"Well, okay," Doris said. "Maybe we can find a pretty spot and stretch our legs."

When they got to exit ten, they took the ramp and all of a sudden they were headed down a beautiful country two lane road. Farms and fields were accented by the incredible blue-green grass and the cows that lazily grazed in the distance. Pretty red barns dotted the landscape.

"It's just like one of those pastoral paintings you see at the mall," John observed.

"Yes," Doris answered. "I'm glad we decided to take the side trip after all."

As they moved on down the road, they didn't meet another car or truck. It was as if nobody was out today enjoying the beautiful weather. "This is a wonderful drive," John stated. "I'd like to get some pictures."

As they drove on, suddenly they came to a small town. John slowed down and finally stopped along the road. "Wait a minute," he said as he drug out his map. "I don't remember a town being on this road." After fumbling around for a while, he laid down the crumpled map in the back seat and looked at Doris. "There ain't no town," John said with a laugh.

"Well, I beg to differ, sir." Doris said with a bit of humor in her voice. "I see one. Or is that a mirage?" Sure enough, in the distance was a town, all right. They drove closer and met a sign that said 'Welcome to Oakville.' They slowly drove on as they began to see side streets, traffic lights, cars parked along the road, stores and shops.

"Let's stop and get a cold drink," Doris requested.

"Sounds like a great idea to me."

Soon, they were in front of the Oakville Drug Store. They parked their car alongside a few more cars and got out. "It's sort of quiet around here," John noticed. "In fact, I haven't seen any moving cars or people walking around."

"Yeah," Doris said as she looked around. "Must be a slow day."

They entered the drugstore and the lights were on. The shelves were stocked and the snack bar appeared to be open for business. However, there was no one in sight. John found a bell at the checkout and rang it. No answer. He rang it again and still silence. "I wonder where everybody is," he mused.

"Well, I'm thirsty," Doris said. "Let's just help ourselves and leave some money on the counter."

"Good idea," John agreed. He went behind the counter, found a couple of paper cups, some ice in the machine, and began to dispense some liquid refreshment. Then he returned to the counter as they both sat down on stools.

"I'll leave a generous amount," he said as he reached in his pocket and laid it gently on the table next to the cash register.

"It's sort of nice but also sort of spooky," Doris said as she started looking over her shoulder. "I feel like someone's watching me."

They finished their drink and walked back outside where they looked around. There was still no sign of people or moving vehicles, although there were plenty parked around the area.

They decided to walk around as they observed more stores. They looked in a few of them. Some were locked and some were open. The grocery store was closed but the shelves were stocked and the lights were on. The food looked fresh.

A service station was open but still no people. The full service bays were open for business and smelled of grease and oil. The gas pumps appeared to be in working order.

They entered a gift shop where they were met with the same enigma as the drug store. They looked around and decided to buy some postcards that had a pretty picture of the welcome sign they had seen. On the back, it said 'Oakville, the Friendly Town.' They laid some money next to the cash register, much more than the price indicated, and left.

John and Doris walked back to their car and decided to ride around some more on the side streets until they met somebody. As they traveled down Main Street, they took a side road called Maple Street. It was aptly named as beautiful large maple trees lined the street. Nice neat houses were next to the road. The yards were freshly and neatly mowed and manicured. Cars were parked in the driveways and garages were full of familiar items such as lawn mowers, garden hoses, bags, tools and toys.

Suddenly, John stopped the car. "Why did you stop?" Doris asked.

"Let's stop at one of these houses and ask someone why the town is so deserted."

"Well, I don't know," Doris responded rather reluctantly. "I feel funny doing that."

"Ah, where's your sense of adventure. Aren't you curious?"

"Sure I am," she said somewhat defensively. "Okay, let's do it."

They pulled into a driveway that had plenty of indicators of inhabitance.

It was a nice single story ranch style, orange brick home with bay windows.

There were two cars in the driveway with a large open garage. A garden in the back seemed to be doing quite well. The corn was tall and it looked like it had been freshly tilled. The yard smelled and looked like it had been freshly mowed. And they were ready to solve this mystery, if indeed there was a mystery to be solved.

They shut off the engine of their car and got out. It looked normal enough, they agreed as they moved toward the front door of this harmless looking home. They knocked on the door but there was no answer. They walked around back and it looked like a typical back yard. A garden hose was poised and ready to water the garden or yard if necessary. Trash cans were next to the wall and flowers were growing under the windows. Still, there was no sign of human life. They knocked on the back door and got no answer.

John knocked again and suddenly the door opened slightly. "I must have knocked a little too hard," he told Doris. "I didn't mean to accidentally open the door."

"I guess it wasn't completely closed," Doris said. As they peered inside briefly, John intended to shut the door gently but before he did, he and Doris happened to see something rather startling. It was an empty house.

"Well, would you look at that," John noticed. He pushed open the door even more. It revealed a large room, completely empty except for lights in the ceiling and curtains on the windows. They could see all the way through to the other side and observed the front door. They could also see their car parked in the driveway through a window between the curtains.

They walked in and looked around, completely amazed at what they saw, or rather what they didn't see. It was like a Hollywood movie set prop. Just then, they heard something at the back door. A large crow had perched himself at the doorway and made a loud cawing sound just before flying off.

"That was an omen," Doris said as they made her way back to the open door. Tiny hairs were standing straight up on her neck.

"Oh, don't be silly," John said with a laugh, slowly following her to the door. "It's just a crow. They're everywhere. He's just looking for food, probably from the garden in the back."

They exited, closed the door tightly so it wouldn't open so easily next time and made their way back to their car in the front. "It sure is strange, though," he related to Doris as he looked around. "I feel like I'm in the middle of a movie set."

They got in their car and continued to ride around, first up Third Street, then Vance Street, stopping along the way to investigate more homes. They were all the same. Completely empty and void of all signs of life except for the birds, butterflies, bugs, and other normal critters.

With nothing else to do and no one to talk to, they decided their time in Oakville was over. It was now time to resume their journey to Aunt Louise's house.

In due time, they arrived in Grantsburg, pulled up to their beloved aunt's house and pecked on the door. A smiling Aunt Louise greeted them cheerfully at the door as she welcomed them in like two long lost friends. "How are you," John asked as they all exchanged hugs.

"Tolerable," she answered. "Sciatica and arthritis, you know. The usual. And you and Doris?"

"Great, thanks." John answered.

"I bet you're starved," John's aunt stated as if she was patiently waiting to offer a feast to a couple of weary travelers.

"As a matter of fact, we are," Doris said. "You see we stopped in a strange little town called Oakville a few miles back and it seemed deserted. We were going to get something there but….." Louise stopped her in mid sentence.

"You stopped in Oakville?" she said with a laugh.

"Yes," John said, a bit confused at here response.

"I'll have to tell you about Oakville." Louise explained. "Sit down, this will take a few minutes. A few years ago an eccentric billionaire named Anson Adams had always had a desire to build and design his own town. Well, he did just that but without people. He built it in the middle of highway forty just off exit ten. The town's not even on the map.

"Yeah, we know," Doris added.

"Then," Louise continued, "He carefully placed cars and stores and shops and had electricity and water brought to the area. He has a whole crew of groundskeepers to keep the place neat and tidy. The houses are empty. He allows the drugstore to be open for passerby to get a drink and the gift shop for tourists to stop and get souvenirs. On certain days the grocery store is open."

"So that's it," John said as he began to see the light.

"You just happened to go there when the maintenance crew was not there. If you go back on Tuesdays and Saturdays, the place is buzzing with all sorts of people doing their jobs keeping the town looking nice. And on Sunday morning, the church bell even rings but there are no people attending. The church is an empty shell. There is security there all the time, watching you. If you'd done something bad, they would have been on you like a robin on a worm."

"Wow," Doris said in amazement. "That's why I felt like someone was watching me. But why go to all that trouble if nobody lives there?"

Louise continued. "He just wanted to build something for people to enjoy without messing it up. You just look around a while and then move on. It's like a tourist attraction."

"You know," John added, "I think I'd like to live there myself."

## Chapter 8

# Philanthropic Pesticides, Inc.

*I*t was that festive time of the year again. The annual Philanthropic Pesticide convention in Botsweegan, Iowa promised to be another success. All seventeen districts were represented and the guest speakers were all lined up at the Bleriott Hotel's convention hall. The hotel's restaurant featured the best local beef, pork, and poultry, and of course, fresh fruits and vegetables. Literature and free samples were always welcome and the farmers and salesmen never failed to go home happy.

The hospitality room was well stocked for the evening and always drew a large crowd. Comparing notes over a drink or two with crackers, nuts, and cheese was always a good way to share ideas and meet new friends. The working farmers, however, were the first to leave the party for they were used to getting up early and going to bed early.

The first morning was always the most exciting as Max Rombo, this year's president of the PPI, made some opening comments. He then introduced the first speaker, Sammy "Bugs" Creacher, and his topic, the 'sandstone technique for sidestepping crop dressing.'

"It's my pleasure to be 'addressing' you this morning," Bugs started out with a chuckle from the crowd. "Or, should I say I believe that the magnificent progress we've made in this field (another chuckle from the savvy crowd) will be covered this morning. It's not been without its pitfalls, to say the least, and I've become wary of the distance we've come in such a short time. Therefore, I'm proposing the legislators to reconsider their ban on digressing pesticide informalities and let us do our own crop dressing, that is to say we must rely on the natural informality of things."

He went on for several more minutes and ended his speech among a standing ovation and a few cheers from the 'amen pew,' closest to the front. In the back a few more cheers were heard.

"Now," Max stated, we shall hear from Terry Sedimen, the soil expert for the district." Terry stepped up to the podium.

"I'll try to be as down to earth as I possibly can," Terry stated the crowd settled down. It was about break time, however, and the group members wanted to stretch their legs. They weren't a crowd that liked sitting still for too long. "I've been soil supervisor in the district for ten years and I believe...."

"Eleven years," someone shouted from the back row.

"How's that?" Terry asked.

"It's been eleven years," the man repeated.

"No," Tom Tuttle said correcting. "Terry's right, it's been ten years and a few weeks."

"Well, whatever," Terry said as he moved from the left side of the podium to the right.

"Get closer to the microphone," Alvin Alexander said. "We can't hear you."

Terry moved to the center of the podium and continued. "Ooops, sorry,"

he said as he grabbed the mike. "Soil is a very serious subject. It's not to be taken lightly, especially when you have clay and loam both on the same strata and you're trying to grow sweet potatoes."

"Here, here," Mike Wikes said from deep within the crowd. "You said a mouthful."

"And therefore," Terry later concluded, "education is the key to good soil management. I believe the median stratum is sitting in the catbird seat, so to speak. We should concentrate on the timely disposal of truncating symbolics."

"What he said!!" Mike spewed from across the room.

After the ten o'clock break, the group took their seats for the next speaker, Mr. Dugan Tuberius, the resident expert on potatoes. He had been around potatoes so long, it's been said, that he even looked like one, rather round and bumpy.

"My long time studies indicate there is a direct relationship between the size of the potato and the amount of fertilizer that's added to the soil. Now you take a scrawny tater compared to a mega spud. You can definitely tell the difference."

Dugan held up two potatoes, one large and one small.

"This poor fellow has been practically starved," Dugan continued. "All he's fit for is throwing in a pot roast baking bag with some carrots and onions."

He then held up a large one.

"On the other hand, here's a class A baker if I ever saw one. I'd be proud to have him on my plate in the finest steak house in Kansas City with a big glob of butter and a dollop of sour cream."

"You certainly know your taters," Phil Hawkins hailed from the center section of the attentive crowd.

The group was having a great time, learning much in the short time they had there. As the afternoon wore on, the last lecture was always a surprise speaker. "And now," Max announced, "for the grand finale of day one, we have Ross Wells for our surprise lecturer."

Mr. Wells even had audio visuals to go with his lecture. He was a short little man with extremely thin hair, thick glasses, a suit that was two sizes too big and black shoes that hadn't been shined in a month. His tie had a mustard stain on it and he looked like a college professor that was lost in the 1950's.

"I'm pleased to be here," Mr. Wells said with a nasally high pitched voice.

"My specialty is crop circles. And you have had some dooszies here in Iowa."

He turned off the lights and started up his overhead projector. It rattled as it threw light onto the screen. His collection of crop circle pictures started off with one that showed different sized interwoven circles that was a real work of art. "As you can see, this couldn't have been done by humans. It had to be done by aliens from outer space."

"Nonsense!!" Chet Pierce shouted from the crowd. "You can even see the tire marks beside them."

The crowd erupted in laughter.

Ross, pausing for a moment and not changing expressions, continued as if nothing happened. He then showed another one with even more elaborate designs than the first. It had squares, triangles, and circles, somehow all masterfully intertwined and flaring off to different angles.

"I see a guy hiding in the weeds with a rake," Chet then interjected.

The crowd was rolling in the aisles.

Ross then turned off his projector, flipped on the lights and stood before the crowd and spoke. "You see, this is exactly the reaction that is expected from a bunch of earthlings."

Suddenly, the crowd saw something moving behind the curtain, obviously trying to find an opening. Finally, it emerged and proceeded toward the podium. It was obviously an "alien" from outer space. It was gray, had long fingers, no ears, short legs, large head and eyes and a small slit for a mouth. The alien's 'skin' appeared to be a rather sloppily fitting rubber suit. It moved slowly toward Mr. Wells.

The crowd was in hysterics, realizing that this was only a joke and a clever and fun way to end the day's lectures. Mr. Wells and his gray friend took a bow as the group responded with a standing ovation. Some were laughing so hard that tears were coming from their eyes.

"Thank you Mr. Wells and friend from…wherever you're from," Max announced as he joined the applause and took the mike. "That concludes the meeting for today. Refreshments will be served in the hospitality room immediately and all are invited. Dinner will be served at 6:00 P.M. As Max looked to the left part of the stage, both Ross Wells and his "alien" friend made their way to the exit. Suddenly, in the blink of an eye as Max looked on, they both seemed to vanish in thin air before they got to the side door. Max just stood and stared for a moment, rubbed his eyes and realized it must have been another trick. 'Better not say anything to the crowd,' he thought to himself. They wouldn't believe it anyway. Besides, it been a long day and he was ready for some of those refreshments, especially a stiff drink.

# Chapter 9

## Sensory Transformation

*A*t the *Good Samaritan Village*, a group home for the intellectually challenged, things were pretty much routine, or as routine as could be expected. One of the long time residents, Ron Peaks, sat at the piano wearing his familiar, slightly tattered blue pullover sweater. He was an elderly slender black man with thin gray hair, He never spoke a word, but played Scott Joplin tunes, along with blues, and songs he had made up.

Helen Carmello, a white lady up in her late-seventies, wore a bluish-gray wig and was knitting a sweater for an imaginary nephew. Unlike Ron, she was a chatterbox, always talking to someone and if no one was around, she just talked to herself. So it was business as usual at Harvey and Alice Kessler's home for the learning disabled.

The residents at this group home for adults had no other place to go. Their ages ranged from twenty-five to eighty-five. They all stayed in the home provided by the Kesslers and their desire to help people less fortunate than themselves. For a variety of reasons, the residents were left here, some because their selfish families wanted them out of the way when keeping them interfered with their free and easy lifestyle. Others were unclaimed victims with no family whatsoever, or at least none that claimed them. Whatever the reasons, they had a safe haven and a comfortable home here, free from expense and worries. The rooms were always clean and warm and they had plenty of good food to eat and no stress. The Kessler's staff saw to that. Their services included nurses and CNAs, cooks and housekeepers, counselors and groundskeepers. A physician was assigned to the home of the twenty-four residents and he visited each patient once a week or more often if needed.

The Kesslers had been independently wealthy when they decided to do something important in their community and with their lives. So, after making a fortune in the real estate business, they bought a large, sprawling estate on the west end of town. Their entire portfolio was tied up in the Good Samaritan Village and with no children of their own, they turned it into a home for their own children, of sorts. A family made up of people others called "intellectually challenged." It didn't matter what others said; they were a happy family with lots of love. They even had a golden retriever named Bosco that wandered in and out of the rooms making the residents feel even more secure and happy. Whatever problems came up, they dealt with them and solved them.

That is until one day Harvey and Alice were visited by their accountant and good friend, Buddy Parker, who happened to be the bearer of bad news that day. "Your expenses have doubled in the past year," he reported. "Within a year you will be broke. It's not your fault and you've done nothing wrong, it's just a sign of the times." It was expensive keeping up twenty-four residents along with paying the staff. And then there was insurance, food, and medical expenses, and the list went on and on. There were taxes, grounds keeping expenses, and repairs to the aging house.

It was a bombshell to the Kesslers, who thought their "fortune" would last them for the rest of their lives. In the past, investments had kept the income flowing like the unstrained mercy that blessed their world. However, with a sagging and depressed economy, low interest rates, and companies declaring bankruptcy, the Good Samarian Home was headed for the breakers, unless something could be done. And it wasn't just them. Other private group homes were suffering the same inevitable fate.

Helen kept on knitting and Ron kept on playing the piano as if nothing was wrong. And in their minds, nothing was wrong. But thanks to a visit from the CPA, the Kesslers found themselves on the wrong end of the checkbook. And if ignorance was bliss, the residents were happy as clams but the Kesslers were doing all the worrying for them.

When word got around to the staff, there was unrest among the troops. They were obviously concerned and some began looking elsewhere for more solid opportunities. After all, there were nursing homes and hospitals where there they would always be needed and the paychecks would always be paid.

Two days after the Kesslers were given the bad news, one of the patients, Jackie Rich had a visitor. His son Kyle, the one who put his father in the group home arrived for a rare visit. He only made it up to the Good

Samaritan about twice a year and Jackie never saw his daughter, older brother or younger sister at all.

Jackie Rich sat in his room most of the time in his wheelchair, staring at the television set. He rarely spoke unless he was agitated about something like changing his catheter or taking a bath. Otherwise, he was content. Everyday they would wheel Jackie to the cafeteria for his meals and then he would sit in the parlor and either stare out the window or listen to Ron's piano playing. The music was the only thing that produced a smile on Jackie's face except for petting Bosco.

After a brief visit, Kyle headed down the steps and was intercepted by Harvey who said he needed to speak to him privately. "Come into my office, Kyle," Harvey said with obvious concern in his voice.

"What's up?" Kyle asked as they entered the small office and closed the door. Suddenly, Helen quit knitting and looked at the closed door. Ron quit playing the piano, cocking his head, squinting his eyes, and also staring at the door.

Inside, Harvey laid the cards on the table. "We're in financial trouble," he started to explain.

"Well," Kyle interrupted before Harvey could elaborate, "I can't take him in. My wife would kill me."

Harvey continued, "I'm not suggesting anything like that. In fact, I knew you wouldn't take in Jackie. All I'm trying to say if that there's a chance that we may have to shut the place down. Expenses have gotten out of control."

"It's not that I don't want him," Kyle explained rather apologetically. "My dad's a lot of trouble and we can't afford to give him the care he needs. Maybe you can find him another place."

"Well," Harvey stated as he rose from his chair. "The responsibility is really on you if he has to go to another place."

"I don't think so," Kyle said as his voice tensed. "I mean I don't know anything about it. Social Services is responsible, aren't they?"

Kyle didn't say another word but got up out of his chair, obviously uneasy, and left the building with not even a goodbye to Harvey Back in the lobby, Helen resumed her knitting and Ron continued his piano playing but kept one eye on Harvey as he went outside to sit on the porch.

"Something's up," Helen said to Ron as he nodded.

"I can just feel it," she explained as she looked at him. "But the Lord will take care of all of us."

As Harvey sat on the porch in a rocking chair, he was suddenly joined by Mary, a longtime resident CNA. She sat beside him. "I know things are not going well," she said, "but you can depend on me to stay. I've been with you since the start and I'm not about to abandon you now, no matter how rough it gets. I've never been in this job for the money and it doesn't really matter to me."

"I really appreciate that," Harvey answered as he stopped rocking. "But I couldn't ask you to stay without being paid. Listen to us; we've already decided that the ship is sinking. Maybe there is a way to keep her afloat."

"I sure hope so," Mary said. "I couldn't live without all my friends here. These wonderful sweet people depend on me."

"They sure do," Harvey said as he resumed his rocking with more vigor. "Maybe there's a way."

In a few minutes, Harvey rose from his chair and went inside. He was stopped by Helen who had gotten up and was standing beside Ron at the piano. "What's the problem?" she asked.

"Oh, nothing, Helen. Don't worry about it. Hey Ronny, how about playing some of that ragtime stuff?"

He put his hands in his lap and looked down at the keys.

"You shouldn't lie to us," Helen said as she looked up at Harvey. "We know something is wrong, don't we Ron?"

"Well," Harvey stated with surprise. "Has someone been telling you things?"

"Nope," Helen answered. "We just know when there's trouble on the horizon." She laid down her knitting.

Harvey had learned that sometimes people who were mentally handicapped had a sixth sense about certain things. Sometimes they could do wonderful things like play the piano or memorize a phone book. Sometimes they could read your mind or predict the future. The unflattering name of "idiot savant" came to his mind as he pondered what else they knew or could do. He preferred to call it "sensory transformation," a way of transferring feelings and senses through other channels.

"All right," Harvey confessed as he tenderly patted Ron and Helen on the shoulders, "we are having financial problems but maybe we can work something out."

"I know we will," Helen said as she looked at Ron who had suddenly started playing Pineapple Rag as Helen smiled, sat back down, and continued her knitting.

Harvey then went upstairs and passed Jackie in the hallway, who was sitting in his wheelchair. "Morning, Jackie," Harvey said as he smiled and waved.

"Listen for the signs," Jackie answered. He never said that before.

"Pardon me?" Harvey inquired as he stopped short.

Jackie clammed up and didn't say another word.

'I wonder what he meant by that?' Harvey thought to himself as he walked away.

Alice and Harvey sat down for lunch and discussed the situation. "I'm really worried," she said. I have really gotten attached to our family here. I'd hate to see it all broken up."

"Yeah," Harvey answered. "You never know what will happen to them at a new place. What if Ron didn't have a piano to play? That's what keeps him going."

"And what about us?" Alice said with concern. "We've been so worried about the people here that we've forgotten that we are, quite literally, the Good Samaritan Village. If it goes down the tubes, so do we. Wouldn't it be ironic if we ended up in the poor house after helping so many people?"

"You're right, Alice. We're going to be broke in a few months unless things improve. And that would take a miracle. There's no relief in sight right now."

Meanwhile, Ron kept playing the piano. Some of the songs he made up were incredibly beautiful. The other residents and visitors were totally amazed at his abilities. Helen kept knitting that sweater for her imaginary nephew and was almost finished. Jackie Rich kept saying softly to himself, "Listen for the signs."

The next morning came and went as Harvey pondered the fate of both his beloved home for the intellectually challenged and for his own fate, which seemed to go hand in hand. His wife Alice was also in a quandary.

Then, Harvey decided to call in his CPA for an emergency conference. About ten o'clock, Buddy Parker arrived with a briefcase full of forms and other papers. He had a solemn look on his face as he entered the front door.

"It's doesn't look good," Buddy said. "It's my professional opinion that you should get out from under as soon as possible."

"Which means?" Harvey asked.

"You should sell out," Buddy quite succinctly stated. "It's the only way to keep from losing everything. Get what you can from this place. But remember, houses are not selling very well right now. It could be a long time before we sold this house and property." Alice looked stunned and shaken but had been expecting this explanation.

Then suddenly, Ron Peaks started playing the piano. It wasn't Scott Joplin, it was something he had made up. It was so beautiful that everyone just stopped what they were doing and just stared and listened. It was as if the angels were taking control of Ron's hands.

"Well, would you listen to that," Buddy said as he rose from his chair and looked out across the lobby. "Who is that?"

"That's Ronny Peaks," Mary said as she wandered by with her towels in hand. "Isn't it beautiful?"

"He's not a resident here, is he?" Buddy asked.

"Yes," Harvey answered. "He's been here a good long while."

"Why is he here and not playing in a concert hall?"

"He's got an I.Q. of 65," Alice stated. "He can't function in society."

"But how can he play like that?" Buddy asked.

"We don't know," Harvey elaborated. "I call it 'sensory transformation,' He never took lessons and he just hears something and can play it. And sometime he makes up songs."

"I can't believe it," Buddy added. "I have a friend in the recording business that needs to hear this."

Without a further word, Buddy left with his briefcase. The next day, a man from a record company, Marco Brunetti, showed up to listen to Ron Peaks tickle the keyboard with his magic fingers. And Ron just happened to be in rare form. The man was mesmerized and could not believe what he was hearing. "It's a miracle," he said. "I've never heard anything like it. I will give him twenty thousand dollars on the spot if he will sign a contract for me. He could make millions."

"He can't sign for himself," Harvey stated as he explained to Marco.

"I see. Then who's his guardian?" the man said.

"I am," Harvey said as he showed the man the legal papers of guardianship.

"Then here's a check for twenty thousand dollars. Much more will come in later when we iron out the details. This is just a down payment."

"The Good Samaritan is saved!!" Mary said as she listened to the miracle unfold. "And Ronny did it for us."

Just then, Helen called Marco over to her and handed him the sweater she'd been knitting. "This is for you, dear nephew," she said as he tried it on.

"It's beautiful, Aunt Helen. And a perfect fit too. Thank you so much."

It was just what they needed to seal the deal.

"I told you not to worry," Helen said as she looked at Ron.

Ron just kept on playing the piano and had a broad smile on his face that no one had seen in a long time.

"He knows," Harvey said to Helen. "He just saved the Good Samaritan."

# Chapter 10

# Who Killed Montague ?

**B**ill Hadley and his friends had just come back to shore after a pleasant day of fishing when they were met by police. They had spent the afternoon cruising up and down the coast trolling for anything that would hook on to their lines and relaxing from the rigors of a stressful work week. Surprisingly, as soon as their thirty foot rented fishing yacht, the Annie Sue, touched the pier, police chief Miles Westrum, his top deputy Andy Cox, and another deputy met them as they started to disembark.

"Did you catch anything?" the chief asked as Bill secured the bow line.

"Not much, Just a couple of croakers and a striped bass," Bill answered, bewildered as to why the police chief was asking him about his afternoon outing.

"Who are your friends?" Westrum inquired.

"Well, this is Brad Norris, lab technician at the hospital," Hadley explained, "Janet Stephens, secretary at the Bon Voyage Travel Agency and my personal friend, and Rance Clarkson, bar tender at the Red Herring Bar and Grill on 43rd Street. What can I help you with?" Bill handed Brad the meager catch of the day in a silver metal bucket.

"A trip downtown for you and your friends for starters," the chief said as another police car pulled up with blue lights flashing, reflecting brightly off the boat.

"What seems to be the trouble?" Janet asked.

"Just a routine check, Miss Stephens," the chief said politely as he touched the brim of his cap. "Something happened today and we need to talk to all of you."

The bewildered fishing quartet piled into two separate cars and headed to the police station where they were put in an interrogation room with a couple of strangers.

"That's them all right," one of the strangers stated as she pointed at the four suspects. "They're the ones shooting at a body in the ocean. We saw them through our binoculars."

"Shooting at a body?" Bill asked, totally surprised as he laughed out loud. "We were just out fishing. You catch fish, you don't shoot them."

Chief deputy Andy Cox then announced, "This is Fred and Edna Wilson. They were in a boat and said they saw you and your crew shoot at something.

"Ah yes," Bill answered, "you were in that boat about a mile from ours. You must have had a telescope."

The police chief then asked, "Who's the leader of this gang?"

"Gang?" Bill replied. "If you're referring to who's in charge of the fishing trip, nobody is."

"A boat without a captain," one of the deputies said as he shook his head, "very strange."

"Do you deny shooting at a person in the ocean?" the police chief asked as he turned on the tape recorder. "Dang, I always forget to turn on this thing."

"We were not shooting at a person," Brad said. "We were shooting at a can in the water to see if we could hit it. We were bored because we weren't catching anything. Then a shark started circling around but we didn't shoot at it."

"Likely story," the witness said with sarcasm. "They were shooting at someone in the water. We saw it moving."

"That must have been the shark you saw moving," Rance added. "After all, you were a mile away. How could you tell what we were shooting at?"

"I bet they killed some guy," Edna surmised, "then threw him overboard and shot him again so the sharks would be sure and eat the evidence."

"Yep, that's what happened all right," Fred added.

"What an imagination," Janet said as she stood up.

"Now now," Miles interjected, "let's don't get into a fight right here in the police station. The fact is that someone has been reported missing. Some old guy that was hanging around the wharf. Then, suddenly he was gone and these people say they saw you shooting at something in the water."

"What old guy?" Bill asked. "What's his name?"

"According to a witness, they thought his name was Jonas Montague, a penniless drifter who liked to go out on boats with strangers who felt sorry for him, drink a few free beers, and maybe get a free catch for his supper or have someone give him a few bucks. Supposedly, he stayed in an old storage shack by the pier. He's not been seen in a couple of days. He was approximately five foot nine, dark greasy hair that stuck out in all directions, brown eyes, ruddy complexion, bushy eyebrows, medium build, short scraggly beard."

"And you think we abducted this old geezer, took him for a ride on the boat, killed him and then dumped his body in the ocean?" Bill said sarcastically, "Just for laughs?"

"We're not accusing you and your friends of anything," the chief said, "but we have to look at all the possibilities. We're waiting for a lab report."

"Lab report on what?" Brad inquired.

"There was blood on the floor of your boat," Andy explained. "We're checking it out."

"Of course there was," Bill stated. "There usually is when you catch and clean fish on a boat."

"We'll see," the chief added.

Just then, another deputy entered the room with a piece of paper in his hand. "Looks like human blood was found on your boat, the Annie Sue, along with fish blood."

"Well, then," the chief said, "the plot thickens. Can you explain that? Now if we can match this blood with that of Montague, we can book this crew of pirates on murder one. Can you explain the blood?"

"Oh yeah," Rance stated with some nervous relief. "I cut my finger on a fish hook and it bled for a while before we could find the first aid kit." He showed them his cut finger and band aid.

Fred and Edna rolled their eyes as they found that story hard to believe.

"It's convenient that you just now remembered that important detail."

"Well that should be easy to confirm," Brad Norris said. "At the hospital lab, we can match up the DNA and confirm Rance's story."

"Maybe," Westrum said.

Unfortunately, through an exhaustive afternoon of searching, there was no official record of Jonas Montague as Bill, Brad, Janet, and Rance, continued to be detained in the downtown police station lobby.

Meanwhile, an interesting development happened that changed everything. A body washed up on shore, riddled with bullet holes and partially eaten by sharks. No bullets were found as they had passed through the body so ballistics could not confirm a match. The body did resemble the description of old Montague but it was badly mutilated so a positive identification could not be made. Same hair color and eyes and approximate height and weight checked out.

"They say the body hasn't been in the water very long," Westrum said as he scratched his chin. "Could have happened this morning."

"See, I told you," Edna said as she looked at Fred, "they are the murderers."

"That's preposterous," Bill said as he jumped out of his chair. "You don't even know if that body is Montague's."

"Lock 'em up," Deputy Cox said as he looked at Chief Westrum. "I'll read them their rights."

"Better get us a lawyer and fast," Janet said to the rest of the suspects.

"I think we'll have to detain you for a while longer," Westrum said. "At least until we can clear this thing up a bit more."

"Oh great," Bill Hadley said, "spend the night in the pokey on circumstantial evidence."

"Pretty strong evidence, if you ask me," Andy added.

So, they waited for the district attorney to make the next move pending some kind of identification of a body that belonged to the alleged Mr. Montague. At the morgue, however, there were other bodies that were unclaimed. Many looked similar to the description of Jonas but as is the case with many derelict street people, friends and relatives don't exactly come out of the woodwork to claim the bodies unless there's an estate involved, which is almost never the case.

"I think we're going to have to let them go," the district attorney said to Chief Westrum. "There just isn't enough evident to charge them. Anyway, the lab work came back that matched Brent's fish hook incident. Same blood type and everything."

"I guess you're right" Miles said. "But I've known a lot of criminals that looked innocent."

"And what about Fred and Edna?" the D.A. asked. "They seemed a bit too anxious to get these folks locked up and charged. That sounded a little suspicious to me."

The next morning, after two deputies spent much of the night snooping around the wharf where Montague was last seen, things took an informative turn. They returned to the station to give a report to chief Westrum. As word got around the neighborhood that someone was missing, it became evident that some of the local folks were indeed talking.

"That's what we need," Miles said as he wrung his hands. "People to tell us some vital information so we can crack this case."

Deputy Shaw then entered the room and gave his report from the previous night's snooping. "Old Lester Mason runs a bait shop just down the pier from that shack where Montague was supposed to be residing. His testimony was that he saw a man hanging around the shack. However, he also stated that he watched the Annie Sue leave port yesterday morning and saw only four people on the boat. The four people matched the description of the four suspects you have in custody."

"Hmmm," the chief said as he scratched his head. "Old Lester knows everything going on around here. I've never known him to lie. And with something as important as this, you know he'd tell us the truth."

Other people came forward with similar stories. Jasper Dillon, a dock worker who'd been around the pier for years said he'd seen a person that fit the description of Jonas Montague. "We get drifters all the time," Jasper stated, "but they all look pretty much the same to me. I mean I don't pay a lot of attention to them. They come and go all the time."

And then, at ten o'clock that morning, Chief Westrum got an important call. "Come down to the morgue," the voice on the office phone said, "we've identified the body that washed up on the shore."

"Now we're getting somewhere," Miles said excitedly as he donned his cap.

When the chief, Andy Cox, and the D.A. arrived at the morgue, they were met by Doctor Phil Hughes, the pathologist.

"He was a gangster," Dr. Hughes stated as he lifted the sheet off the body. "Alfredo Marconi was his name but he went by 'Two Gun Marconi.' You've seen his picture in the newspaper. Apparently, he tried to rat on his friends and was disposed of in the usual manner. He was shot multiple times then taken out to sea, and dumped into the ocean, probably in the middle of the night. The bullet holes were from a 9 mm instead of a .38 special, which is what the type of gun the Hadley group had. And as you can see, what the sharks didn't eat, the rest washed up on shore."

"Ooh, yuck," the D.A. stated with disgust as he covered his nose with his handkerchief.

"Cover up the stiff," the police chief pleaded. "We've seen enough.

I guess that clears the fishing party, at least for now. Release them immediately. We're right back to square one though. "We still are missing one Jonas Montague."

Two days went by as more people were interviewed. If time heals all wounds it doesn't do any favors to the memory. After thinking about it for a while, Lester Mason came into the police station and announced that he thought he'd seen Montague wandering around the docks that morning, alive and well. Jasper Dillon and Pete Crumbley both saw two other men who looked like Jonas Montague the night before. Soon, reports were coming in from all over town.

"We must be dealing with a ghost," Chief Westrum said to his deputy as he twisted his hair into a knot on top of his head.

"Sure looks that way," Deputy Cox said in agreement as he chuckled. "How many Montagues do you suppose there are anyway?"

Chief Miles Westrum and his office staff were soon in for a shock, however.

Suddenly a man walked into the office who looked exactly like the missing person, from the scraggly beard to the ruddy complexion to the bushy eyebrows. Westrum jumped up out of his seat as if he'd seen a ghost and immediately confronted the rough looking gentleman. "What's your name?" he asked accusingly.

"Jonas Montague," the man blurted, somewhat taken aback by the verbal inquisition. "I just came in to ask if I could borrow your restroom?"

"That's impossible?" the deputy asked.

"You don't have a restroom?" the man asked.

"You got any I.D.?"

"Nope," the man said. "I haven't had a driver's license in years. I just need to use your restroom for a minute. And a cup of that coffee would be nice too."

"Go ahead," Westrum said as he pointed to the restroom door, looking a bit pale.

The man quickly returned from the restroom looking refreshed. "Thanks a lot," he said. "By the way, I understand someone's been looking for me."

"Where do you live?" the chief asked.

"Down by the docks in a storage shack. But I'm moving soon."

"We've all been looking for you," the chief finally answered. "We thought you were dead."

"Really? I had to leave for a couple of days to visit my cousin up in Bridgeton. He's got a job for me in his hardware store. It doesn't pay much but it's a job and I can stay in the furnished upstairs room. I just came back to get my things."

"You've caused quite a stir around here," Westrum explained.

"Sorry about that. It's nice to know so many people are interested in my well being."

"After you disappeared, people have been seeing Jonas Montagues all over the place," Cox stated.

"Really? That's interesting. But how do you know there are not more of me, sort of like an army of clones that are planning to take over the world?" Montague paused, then laughed. "Just joking."

Jonas' laugh sent chills down Westrum's back and caused Andy to spill his coffee on his white shirt.

"Yeah, that's funny," Westrum added. "Have a nice day. You'll like Bridgeton. It's a nice town."

"Oh, here's your coffee," Andy said as he handed Jonas a plastic cup full.

"Thanks," Mr. Montague said as he carefully carried it with him toward the door.

Jonas then left the police station and disappeared behind a warehouse as Westrum and Cox watched him from the window.

"I guess we now know who killed Montague," Chief Westrum said as he turned and looked at his chief deputy.

"Yeah," Andy Cox added. "Nobody killed Montague."

In the weeks that followed, however, they kept a sharp lookout around town to be sure there were no more Jonas Montagues lurking in the midnight shadows.

Meanwhile, Fred and Edna Wilson, not completely satisfied about the explanation they got from the police, staked out around the wharf while they took pictures of various transient derelicts. On one occasion, however, their camera met a trip into the harbor when a man that fit the description of Jonas Montague grabbed it and tossed into the water.

# Chapter 11

# Matt Starr —Space Detective

As Matt Starr sat in his favorite café, *The Greasy Comet*, he sipped a cup of coffee, nibbled a honey bun pastry, and hastily flipped through the pages of a day old newspaper. The nights in Skytropolis could be long and boring when you're a private detective looking for work. The city was just about cleaned up, thanks to chief of police Oswald Axis, who had made a point of cracking down on crime in the city. The point was well taken and Matt was thinking about looking for another line of work if the crime rate didn't pick up. Besides, honey buns and coffee cost money and he hardly had enough Krons to pay his rent.

'Things could be a lot worse,' he philosophized to himself, pondering his lack of money. He picked up a fly swatter.

"I hate Axis and his cops," he said to the waitress as she walked over to his table with the check. "He's killing my business."

"The business ain't too great here either," she responded as she chewed greedily and loudly on her chewing gum.

Matt thought about his days as a student of the Skytropolis Private Detective Academy, a mail order course, which he affectionately called "Gumshoe U." He sailed through the required twelve lessons in only six weeks and got his diploma. He had worked on several cases in the private sector but business had all but come to a grinding halt.

"Maybe I should have been a short order cook,' he thought as he swatted at a fly that landed on the booth. He missed.

"Another bun, honey?" the waitress asked in a joking manner as she chewed gum, popping a bubble inside her mouth.

"No thanks, Rosie," Matt responded as he folded up the newspaper and tossed it into an empty booth, missing the seat as papers slid to the floor. "I can't afford it." He gave her a Kron tip and politely said, "Keep the change." Out of the corner of his eye, he saw a cockroach scurry across the floor. 'It's the big ones I'm after,' he thought to himself. He took out his Fogmo-64 laser gun and blasted the insect, leaving a small crater in the tile.

"Quit doing that!" a voice bellowed from the kitchen. Buzzy Fitch, the owner, did not think the firearms display was amusing. "You still owe me for a cup of coffee and a honey bun from the other day."

"Try to do somebody a favor," Matt yelled to Buzzy. "Don't worry, I'll pay you when my ship comes in." He then left the café.

The Greasy Comet was only a block away from his home, the Nova Street Apartments. His room number was 328. Matt walked up the street, dimly lit thanks to kids who had accidentally broken out one of the overhead lights during a street ball game. 'It's hard to get the maintenance department to do anything on this end of town,' Matt thought to himself as he kicked a can.

He was in the habit of noticing everything around him because it was the essence of being an investigator. It was something he learned in detective school but sometimes he saw things that seemed suspicious but usually turned out to be nothing. His overactive imagination conjured up clues to crimes that hadn't been committed. However, along Nova Street, crimes could be a dime a dozen if you only saw the right merchandise. And it was usually hot.

This was not an upscale neighborhood but it was all Matt could afford, at least for the time being. Dogs barked occasionally day and night as they stood guard around the neighborhood, watching out for intruders.

Not that there was anything here worth intruding.

Cats patrolled the streets in the wee hours of the night as they looked for rats that seemed to be taking up residence along the sidewalk trash cans. It was the human rats that Matt was after.

As he neared his apartment, he noticed a big shiny black car parked across the street. At least it looked black in the dim light. 'They must be lost,' he thought to himself. 'Not a good place for a big expensive auto to be at night. It looks like a brand new Streakster-77. Even in the dim light, its large fins sparkled like diamonds. And diamonds are often stolen - especially around here.

Two men sat in the car as two pairs of eyes watched Matt proceed to the apartment steps. 'I wonder what they want in this sleazy neighborhood?' he wondered. 'Maybe they need a detective, who knows.'

He walked to the third floor and put the key in the lock of number 328, opened its squeaky wooden door and entered. In the dark he glanced at his telephone from a distance and noticed it was not blinking. 'Bad sign,' he thought to himself. It was apparent that no one had left a message on his answering machine. He flipped on the overhead light. He could see his detective diploma against the wall over his desk. It was a little dusty.'This room could use a good cleaning out,' Matt thought to himself. 'Too bad Skytropolis doesn't need one too.'

Through his window he heard two car doors close. He looked out and saw the two men from the black Streakster as they proceeded toward the Nova Street Apartments. The dogs started barking and the cats started to scurry.

'Hmmm,' he thought, 'the plot thickens. I think I'll wait up a while and see what develops. With a car like that, they must have a lot of money to spend on a private detective's expert services.'

Matt Starr was six feet tall with a slender build. He had bushy curly dark hair and a full mustache. He wore a loosely fitting, rather randomly arranged necktie around the open collar of a cheap white shirt. His snub nosed Fogmo-64 laser gun lived in a holster attached to his belt and was hidden by his jacket. The Fogmo-64 was considered obsolete but, fortunately, was never used by Matt except for an occasional session of target practice on cockroaches.

After about ten minutes, Matt gave up on the two strangers and started to settle down for the evening. 'Might as well watch an old detective movie. Might learn something.' He turned on the television set and scanned the channels.

Just then there was a knock on the door. Matt got up and went toward it. 'Must be the landlord,' he thought, 'begging for money. Can't get blood out of a turnip. He'll just have to wait.'

Matt opened the door.

Two men stood in the doorway wearing expensive black suits and smelling of cheap cologne. One was tall and one was short. 'Sort of a comical looking pair,' Matt thought to himself as he chuckled out loud.

"You Matt Starr?" the short one asked bluntly. He had an ugly bulldog-like scowl on his face.

"Guilty," Matt answered as he raised his hands. "You need a detective? I have a special this week. Only forty Krons for the first day, then only ten Krons a day..."

"Shut up," the tall one said rudely as he pushed Matt back inside his apartment.

"Too expensive?" Matt asked as he straightened his shirt. "Maybe we can work out a cheaper fee."

The two men entered Matt's apartment without being invited and closed the door behind them so other tenants couldn't hear them talk.

"Let's go for a ride," one of the men said as he brandished a nasty looking NUK-94 automatic pistol, sometimes called a 'mini-nuke.' It had a twenty round banana clip. "The boss wants to talk to you."

"It's kind of hard to go anywhere with the door closed," Matt said with a nervous smile but sensing he was up to his dusty diploma in impending doom. "Besides, I'm not really Matt Starr. He lives down the street."

"I'll take the heater," the short man said as he pulled the sidearm from Matt's holster.

"What's this?" the tall one said with a laugh. "An old Fogmo-64? I didn't know there were any of these antiques around any more."

"I was going to upgrade it to a 64-A when I got enough money," Matt said with a wry smile.

"Don't say another word," the short man said as he aimed his NUC-94 at Matt's temple, "or you'll become a small mushroom cloud."

"That sounds sort of like a threat," Matt responded.

"Shut up," the tall one barked.

"What's this all about?" Matt asked as the two men ushered him out the door. They did not answer as they all hustled him down the steps.

Outside, another pair of eyes was getting into the act. Behind a light pole and across the street was a woman who observed the whole ordeal.

Meanwhile, the two men shoved Matt into the back seat as the tall one got behind the wheel and the short one sat with Matt, making sure the NUK-94 was trained on him every second.

"Hey," Matt said, "I've never been in one of these before. Nice car. Did you pay cash or make payments?"

"Quiet!!!" the man in the front snapped rudely.

"If you need a private detective," Matt said nervously, "I can recommend a lot of good ones."

"Shut up, I said," the driver barked again as he glanced back and glared at Matt. "If he says another word, gag him." The short man did not answer but kept his sinister bulldog expression.

They drove quickly down Nova Street, took the ramp onto Starlight Boulevard and went about a mile and a half. Then they exited onto

Phoebe Street. After a few blocks, they were in a much better part of town. Skytropolis had a lot of nice areas and this was just on the outskirts of Stardust Boulevard, one of the ritzy parts of the city.

They pulled into a driveway and got out. It was a nice two story house and somehow Matt felt that he was the guest of honor.

The weapon was still trained on Matt's head and his gut instinct was that this was the end of the line for the best detective that Skytropolis ever had. Whatever he had done to make these people mad was a mystery for he did not recognize them and hadn't been involved in any cases for weeks. He wanted to find out, not that it would do him any good now - unless he could talk his way out.

They all exited the car and proceeded toward the house. The two thugs looked around to make sure they hadn't been followed. "The coast is clear," The driver said as they went up the walkway.

They entered the building into a lobby where two more guards were watching with guns drawn. "The boss is waiting for you upstairs," one said. "What took you so long?"

"He lives in a dump," one of the gunmen said, "and he stayed at that rat infested café longer than we thought he would."

"I wish I'd stayed longer," Matt said profoundly.

"I hope we didn't get any fleas while we were in that apartment building," the short one said as he scratched his arm.

'Fleas really like rats,' Matt thought to himself.

"Upstairs," the tall one ordered as he pointed. "The boss is getting corns on his elbows from waiting so long."

They entered a room where a short and rather plump, well dressed man sat behind a desk. He had a wide mouth with big lips and was wearing an expensive pin stripe black suit with a red rose boutonniere. He had a white silk handkerchief sticking neatly out of the breast pocket. His face was red as if he were blushing and his greasy black hair was beginning to gray along the temples. He had a large blunted nose and bushy eye brows. On each side of him were two guards wearing black wide lapel suits, holding guns. 'They look like bouncers in a second rate night club, wearing cheap suits and smelling of cheap cologne,' Matt thought to himself as he looked at the rotund fellow behind the desk.

"This is the end of the line for you, punk," the boss said with a rather sinister smile. Matt noticed a large diamond on the man's right hand that was the largest he'd ever seen.

"What have I done to offend you?" Matt inquired.

"It's not what you did," the man said, "it's what you know."

"And what is that?" Matt asked. "I've never been accused of knowing too much."

One of his cronies aimed his gun at Matt. "Goodbye, Matt Starr. You third rate gumshoe dropout."

Just then, the door flew open, obviously helped by a foot that struck it hard like a sledge hammer. It was Sharkey LeGrand, world famous space patrol officer and former pirate brandishing two particle beam weapons, one in each hand like a gunfighter in the Old West.

"I wouldn't be saying goodbye to Matt Starr just yet," Sharkey said as he began firing rounds, striking the man behind the desk with a powerful stream of radiation, who crumpled face first on his desk. Then in a split second, Sharkey had shot the other two men, who fell to the floor like lifeless rag dolls. Matt never knew anyone could fire a hand held weapon that fast and accurately. Wilma, Stretch, and Bobo, then entered the room to make sure Sharkey was all right.

"What the heck is going on here?" Matt asked as he looked at his would be assassins. "I didn't get a chance to tell him I was not a dropout."

Sharkey introduced himself and his three friends. "You happened to be in the wrong place at the wrong time, Matt."

"It's the story of my life," he answered.

"Yeah," Wilma said, "it's a good thing we found you."

"Hey, I know you people," Matt said, a bit surprised. "You work for the Space Patrol. I've seen your pictures in the newspaper and on T.V. How did you find me?"

Sharkey looked at Matt, then Wilma, Stretch, and Bobo, and said, "We just followed the cheap cologne." They all had a good laugh except Matt who was still in the dark.

Three policemen then entered the room to handcuff the crumpled suspects.

"They'll wake up in a few minutes, unharmed," Sharkey explained to Matt. "Then the police will take them off to jail in a paddy wagon waiting outside. Attempted murder, kidnapping, extortion, and a few other charges ought to earn them a trip to Hard Rock Penitentiary for a good many years."

"What about the two thugs downstairs?" Matt inquired.

"Oh," Wilma answered, "we stunned them when we came in the front door."

Matt then looked at Sharkey's weapon and identified it as a BM-88-B particle beam weapon, the elite side arm of the Space Patrol. It is officially known as a 'Blast Master 88-B.'

"Wow," Matt said, "I'd like to have one of those."

"It has a stun feature," Sharkey explained, "among other things. We wanted these rascals alive."

"Who was the big guy behind the desk?" Matt asked.

"We'll let Inspector Locknose explain everything to you later," Sharkey ordered. "He and Chief Axis want to talk to you downtown right now and we'd better not keep them waiting."

"Yeah," Wilma added, "they are always in a bad mood about something."

They left the building and got into a police car, a Flashbolt Ultra 98.6, then sped off into the dimly lit Skytropolis suburbs toward the heart of the brightly lit city.

# Chapter 12

# Mr. Big

Matt was in the middle of a whirlwind tour of emotions. Could this be a dream from watching too many detective shows? A lot happened in a short time and it could be the longest dream of his life. But dreams sometimes turn into nightmares. He pinched himself and determined he was awake.

They finally arrived at Space Patrol headquarters where Chief Axis and Inspector Locknose were waiting. Sharkey, Bobo, Stretch, and Wilma, were there too. They all took a seat.

"I know you are wondering what has just happened," Axis said as he looked at Matt. "You've been part of a sting operation. You indirectly helped us catch one of the biggest criminals in the galaxy. I'll let Inspector Locknose fill you in on the details."

Matt wondered why the local police and the Space Patrol were working together on a case but figured there were a lot of things he didn't know.

The Inspector addressed the group and took charge as he usually did, "When Chief Axis says 'big,' he's not exaggerating. In fact, we call him 'Mr. Big' and he is actually a galactic criminal who found that Skytropolis was a nice place to hide and to run some of his illegal businesses. You ran into him and some of his cronies tonight."

"They'll do a lot of time in jail," Axis interjected. "Probably Sky Slab Prison in the third quadrant."

"Pretty slick," Matt added. "But what did all this have to do with me?"

"Word got out, so they thought," Locknose said, "that you were in contact with one of his rival gangs from the planet of Torvaleda, only sixty light years from here."

"You've got to be kidding," Matt said with a nervous laugh. "I had nothing to do with them and I never heard of that planet."

"Galactic crime seems to be a widespread problem," Sharkey added.

"Even in Skytropolis. And sometimes innocent people like you get caught up in it."

"I can believe that," Matt responded. "I somehow feel like I'm part of a some big puzzle."

"Sort of," Axis quickly stated. "You have been frequenting a night spot called 'Club O'Weird' on the east end of town. You have been talking to a big time galactic racketeer named Thomas 'the Ace' Mace. Word got around through the usual channels that you were in company with this thug who just happens to be an enemy of Mr. Big, who thought you were one of Mace's colleagues."

"And Mace is from Torvaleda?" Matt inquired.

"Yes," Sharkey answered.

Chief Axis continued, "Then they planned to have you rubbed out as part of a down payment on the payback plan. You little trip to that house was part of the ruse. After they turned you into an unrecognizable pile of burned out ashes with a NUC-94, they were going to send your remains to Mr. Mace, C.O.D. with no return address and no bill."

"The rest was simple," Locknose added. "We just waited them to nab you so we could follow them to the house, which was their hideout."

"But how did you know I was being kidnapped? There was nobody outside on the street?"

"We had someone hidden out there," Axis stated. "And you're about to meet her."

"Her?" Matt answered.

Out of a back door entered a tall, dark haired, woman with black penetrating eyes and a sly smile.

"I must have been blind not to see her," Matt stated as he came up out of his chair. "I'm always willing to help out the Space Patrol."

"Permit me to introduce myself," the girl said. "I'm Crystal Moon, special Space Patrol agent."

"I can believe that," Matt said as his eyes were fixed on the tall glass of water named Crystal.

"How would you like working for the Space Patrol?" Inspector Locknose asked Matt. "We need a detective to work out in the field."

Matt's eyes lit up and he saw a golden opportunity for advancement but couldn't help but think Crystal Moon was like the carrot in front of the goat, leading it to the slaughter house.

"Crystal would be your assistant, of course," Locknose added.

This final bonus was too good to pass up, Matt thought. And the money might be secondary.

Matt thought hard to see how he became a piece of the puzzle and it started to fall into place. He tried to connect the dots as it seemed he was the only one in the room who didn't know the score of this bizarre intergalactic game that Inspector Locknose, Chief Axis, and Sharkey and his Space Patrol cronies were playing.

Matt remembered the last time he was in his favorite after midnight hangout, Club O'Weird. Who did he meet from the cosmic underworld but didn't realize? Someone with connections, no doubt. And the dots were beginning to come together.

It had been a hot and steamy night, to say the least, and performing was Pig Man Maxwell and the Atomizers, who were putting on a real show. Maxwell came out on stage dressed up like a big hog and two women were beside him with atomizers. They would spray water on him as he dripped and sang his way through his performance:

"I'm sweating like a pig, my friend,
But please don't get me wrong,
It ain't no fun being hot and wet
When I'm trying to sing this song, my friend,
When I'm trying to sing this song, my man
Just please don't get me wrong."

Then the two girls would sing as they held their noses:
"Oh me...Oh my...You smell just like a sty,
No time to stand around and sniff,
Just quickly say goodbye, my friend,
Just quickly say adieu my man,
No time to stand around."

The girls would frantically spray him heavily with water and the

Pig Man would continue to sing and drip to the delight of the crowd, slinging water in all directions:

"When the bullets start to fly, my man,
You'd better hit the deck,
Cause when the pig man slings some sweat
There's gonna be a wreck, my friend,

There's gonna be a wreck, my man,
If you don't hit the deck."
And the girls would spray and sing again:
"Oh phew, abhor....you smell just like a boar,
Don't pause or stop or even look,
Just hurry toward that door, my friend,
Just scurry toward that door, my man,
Don't even stop and look."

This went one for several more verses when suddenly a man sat down at Matt's table. He was dressed in a white suit with a big black tie and an purple orchid boutonniere. He smelled of expensive cologne and cheap cigar smoke. He snapped his finger and a waiter brought both of them a fresh martini.

"He's pretty bad, isn't he?" Matt said as he looked at the man.

"I've seen better," he responded.

"Yeah," Matt answered. "But the girls are cute."

"Would you like to meet one of them later?" the man said. "I can arrange for you to meet Miss Dusty Capri, the blond bomb."

"I'd like to meet either one of those girls," Matt instinctively blurted.

"How much money do you have on you?" The man asked.

"Five Krons," Matt answered apologetically. "But I have a few more in a shoe box in my apartment."

The man paused for a moment, then spoke, "Forget it." He then got up, patted Matt on the back and walked away.

That's about all he remembered about his last trip to Club O'Weird.

Matt snapped out of his little trip down memory lane, "I bet Miss Capri wouldn't even give me the time of day anyway."

"Who?" Wilma asked.

"Forget about her," Sharkey interjected. "She's not your type."

"The story of my life," Matt added. "But he must have been the one."

"Who?" Stretch asked.

"The guy that was trying to set me up with Miss Capri. Thomas 'the Ace' Mace?"

"Yeah," the Chief Axis said, "while the walls had eyes you were were focused on Miss Capri. It was Mace and he owned that night club.

We've busted him. He's already in jail."

"You guys move fast," Matt stated.

Chief Axis walked around his desk and stood directly in front of Matt as he looked him squarely in the eyes.

"We want to talk to you about a job."

"Sorry, I can't afford to put on an assistant right now," Matt answered. "Just kidding."

"I'm listening," Matt added as he got more serious. Axis continued without cracking a smile.

"We need an agent to travel into the galaxy and investigate certain questionable activities."

Locknose added, "You've already had a taste of some intergalactic thugs. What do you think?"

"As long as Sharkey and his pals are around to help," Matt answered with a smile.

"I wish they could," the chief stated, "but they won't always be there to help. They have their own duties."

Matt got more serious and responded, "I think I might like that job. But why me?"

"We've done some checking on you," Axis explained. "You have experience as an investigator. You handled yourself well tonight. You've never been busted. And you need the job."

"That pretty well sums it up," Matt answered. "When do I start?"

"Go home, get a good night's sleep, and then report to us tomorrow morning," Axis said. "Then we'll take care of your apartment and your belongings. Soon, you will be moving to better quarters."

"It's beginning to sound better all the time," Matt added.

"There's something you need to know about your new colleague, Miss Moon," Locknose added.

"She's married, right?" Matt said sardonically.

"Nothing like that," Axis quickly reacted.

"I hate to break the news to you, Matt," Locknose said with a speck of remorse, barely detectable. "But she's not exactly a real person."

"I beg your pardon," Matt said with some confusion.

"She's one of Professor Overbright's little experiments," Locknose added with a wry smile. "You have heard of him, haven't you?"

"Of course," Matt said. "He's just about the smartest scientist in the galaxy."

"Not all of his experiments have turned out this beautifully," Bobo added with a smile.

Locknose squeezed a tendon on the back of her neck and the top of her head popped open, revealing a neatly arranged group of flashing micro circuits and wires.

"What the…." Matt said as he hopped up and looked for himself, peering down her cranial cavity that should have been filled with gray matter. "I knew she was too good to be true."

"Maybe I shouldn't have said that she's not exactly human, Locknose clarified. "I wouldn't want to hurt her feelings. And she does have feelings, but only in a protective sense."

He closed her lid.

"It's beginning to sound a little bizarre," Matt answered as he settled back into his chair.

"She can be programmed to be your partner," Sharkey said. "She can think for herself, fire a weapon, protect you, and reason. Just like a real person."

"You've just hired yourself a space detective," Matt said as he shook the hands of Locknose and Axis. "I'll be here tomorrow morning." They drove Matt back to his apartment.

All the details were settled and Matt Starr was signed on as the new space detective. He couldn't believe his good fortune as he started a grueling eight week training session. Sharkey and his crew were assigned to do the training and Matt's new spaceship, the *Cosmic Cobra*, was a close copy of Sharkey's Dragon but with a few minor changes.

It was equipped with the latest weapon, the Riptron II and Matt had his own BM-88-B hand held weapon, the mere thought of which would scare the pants off most galactic criminals. Unlike the Dragon, the Cosmic Cobra had a crew of three instead of four. It consisted of his robotic assistant, Crystal Moon, who was also the weapons specialist. and Dusty Monzok, the pilot navigator. They were all cross-trained so they could do any of the other's jobs. Together they worked hard at learning the new spaceship, putting in long hours. Matt didn't think being a space detective involved so much work.

It not only required a concerted effort to learn all the details of space ship technology plus an encyclopedic wealth of knowledge about many other things including the galaxy itself, criminal activities, laws, self defense, weapons, and ways to be sneaky without getting caught.

Dusty Monzok was a veteran of the Space Patrol and former pilot of the ship Quasar II. He was highly recommended by Sharkey and his crew. He was also fearless, intelligent, and a great fighter. Cool under pressure, he was average height and build with jet black hair.

As the time got closer for their first practice mission, Matt was called into Locknose's office for a conference with Sharkey and his crew. "It's about time for a solo," the inspector explained. "However, we have that crisis in Torvaleda. You will have to go it alone, that is to say with Dusty and Crystal."

"What are you trying to say?" Matt said as he sat up in his chair.

"You're on your own," Sharkey explained. "We were going to go with you on a practice mission then set you adrift on your own, but something came up. We won't be able to be with you for a while. Looks like on the job training for you now."

Matt gulped hard and looked at the inspector. "By the way, what am I supposed to do?"

"You'll get a briefing tomorrow morning, then you and your crew will head for Torvaleda. According to intelligence reports, some of Mr. Big's associates are planning to attack Skytropolis. The head of the Torvaleda branch is called Demonius Rex. Your job is to stop him and his associates any way you can."

"Dead or alive?" Matt asked.

"You got it." The Inspector said calmly.

Matt headed back to his quarters with the realization that he was in this up to his diploma in thugs and there was no turning back now. The future of Skytropolis might very well depend on his success or failure, and on his very first mission. He did have the satisfaction of knowing that Crystal Moon and Dusty Monzok were there to help. But it wasn't help that he needed, it was a miracle. And miracles were about as plentiful as honest people in his Nova Street neighborhood. Ah, for the simple days of honey buns and coffee at the Greasy Comet.

Soon, after miracles never came, Matt and his two associates were on the launch pad ready to take off through that magical opening through Skytropolis' canopy that would send him to that distant planet known as Torvaleda.

# Chapter 13

# The Starring Role

*I*n this sealed envelope are your orders," Inspector Locknose stated as Matt and his crew boarded the Cosmic Cobra. "As soon as you clear the Skytropolis canopy, open it up and read it to your crew."

Matt took the envelope and looked at the inspector. "If I don't return, would you pay my bill at the Greasy Comet? I still owe them for a honey bun and a cup of coffee."

"Sure thing," the inspector said with a wry smile. "You still have time to back out if you don't think you're quite up to it."

"Don't worry about me," Matt said with all the confidence he could muster under the circumstances.

"It's not you I'm worried about," the inspector answered, "it's the safety of Skytropolis. Just kidding."

Matt entered the Cosmic Cobra and did all the things he was taught. Sharkey and his crew were excellent teachers and he had wished they were there to see him off but they were on official business elsewhere in the galaxy. At least they could have encouraged him by pushing him into the spaceship.

"Ready for systems check," Dusty Monzok announced as they strapped themselves in their seats. "Ah, don't worry about a thing, we'll be fine - I hope."

"Sure," Crystal said as her eyes twinkled. "I'm programmed to take care of any situation. Well, almost any."

"That's easy for you to say," Matt said as he heard a rumbling sound from the TXQ-35-A1 motor as it started revving up.

Dusty went through the check list and all systems were working perfectly. Suddenly, they were off the launch pad and rising up through the atmosphere above Skytropolis. Then a section of the canopy opened up as they skillfully exited through it. They were now in outer space, leaving dear old Skytropolis behind.

When they were safely away, Matt took the envelope and opened it. "Here it is folks, the mission for the day."

Crystal and Dusty gave their attention to Matt as he continued. "Change direction to 94 degrees from vector 183. Sixty light years to planet Torvaleda. Enter atmosphere at 17 degrees from vector 106. The NavTrek3000 will be programmed to land you in a remote area. Await further instructions there."

Soon, Skytropolis faded into the distance and disappeared. It was now up to the crew of the Cosmic Cobra to stop Mr. Big's associate known as Demonicus Rex. They accelerated to a speed called 'slick 60,' or sixty times the speed of light. As fast as this is, it was still not fast enough. It would still take a year to reach their destination. Fortunately, the Cosmic Cobra had Atomic Compression and could achieve even higher speeds by using infinity as a medium of travel. In a matter of minutes, they were approaching Torvaleda.

"Activate Sky Block," Matt ordered as Dusty flipped some switches. Sky Block enabled them to enter the atmosphere of Torvaleda un-noticed by creating an extreme electromagnetic field around the ship. This caused the Cosmic Cobra to be invisible to the naked eye. They also had 'personal sky block,' utilized by their BM-88-B weapon, enabling them to invisibly walk around away from the ship after they landed.

They entered the atmosphere of their destination at the designated co-ordinates and could see a city below. Following the prescribed directions they landed in an open vacant lot, totally invisible to any inhabitants that might be looking that way.

"Phase two," Matt said as he read more from the mission Axis had given to him.

"Proceed to 822 Torch Street on the west end of the city. This is his headquarters. It is about a mile and a half from your landing zone."

"Sounds simple enough so far," Crystal stated with some confidence.

"Anything else?" Monzok asked.

"Nope, that's it," Matt added. "I guess we're on our own. With the personal sky block, we should be able to wander in that building and take care of Demonicus Rex."

So they left the ship and walked up a series of streets until they came upon Torch Street. They followed it to number 822 and saw that it appeared to be a warehouse with a locked door. No sign was posted and it looked deserted.

"Shall we bust in?" Dusty Monzok asked his colleagues.

"I don't think that would be such a good idea," Matt answered as he pulled something out of his pocket. It was a device for picking locks that he got while he was in detective school. "I think this would be the best approach to get inside."

He skillfully picked the lock and it opened easily. "Be quiet," Monzok stated. "Although they can't see us, they can hear us and although we are invisible, we still have mass, which is detectable by radar. In other words, we're still vulnerable to injury."

As they entered the warehouse, they followed a hallway to a series of rooms. Then they heard talking inside one of the rooms. They stopped nearby and listened.

"I think we should attack Skytropolis as soon as possible. They're bound to send some Space Patrol people to look for us. You're right, Demonicus, the sooner the better. But how do you plan to destroy Skytropolis. Use your head man, we don't have the means to destroy the whole planet but we can attack it with suicide ships. We can sure cause a lot of damage. And they can't trace it back to us. Besides, by the time they react, we'll be gone to our hideout on Arcturus 6. Good thinking, Demonicus."

"So that's it," Monzok whispered to Crystal and Matt. "They just plopped the whole plan right in our laps. This is great."

"It sounds too good to be true," Matt answered. "Here we are right in the middle of the beehive."

"Let's get them," Crystal said excitedly.

"No," Matt answered. "We need to learn more."

Suddenly, they were no longer invisible. "What the..." Monzok said as they heard a voice behind them.

"Drop your weapons," the voice said. They had to oblige as their cover was blown.

Demonicus and two cronies came out of the office and were less than pleased to see the intruders. "Well, what have we here? Spies among us or perhaps some Space Patrol goons from Skytropolis that have come to arrest us?"

"You got the drop on us Tex," Matt said. "But how did you know we were here and how did you neutralize our invisibility?"

"We're not stupid," Demonicus said. "We have ways of detecting you and we have discovered how to neutralize your so-called 'personal sky block.' Put them in the dungeon until I decide what to do with them. I might be able to get some valuable information later."

They were escorted below where they were searched for other weapons and were then put into a jail cell.

"Now what?" Monzok asked dejectedly.

"It looks rather hopeless," Crystal said to Matt. "Unless you have any bright ideas."

"I may have another trick or two up my sleeve," Matt answered. "After all, I learned a lot in detective school."

Hidden in the sole of his shoe was a small glass vial. Inside the vial was some highly concentrated acid. He opened the vial and poured it into the lock. Suddenly, fumes started rising and a sizzling sound was heard.

"There, that ought to do the trick," he told Monzok and Crystal. In a few seconds, it melted the locking mechanism and they were able to easily open the cell door.

"Very clever," Crystal said. "Now what?"

Inside the other shoe was another vial. He secured it and told the rest of them to proceed up the steps. "What's in that vial?" Dusty asked.

"A gas that will temporarily knock them out," Matt answered. "When we meet them down the hall, I'll toss this onto the floor, it will break open, releasing the gas. Simply hold your breath until they are unconscious and then we'll get our weapons back. We'll deliver them to the Skytropolis Space Patrol and we'll have succeeded in our mission."

They stealthily worked their way down the hall until they heard the familiar voices. "Now that we got those snoopers out of the way, we can proceed with operation 'Skytropolis Meltdown.' But first, we need to get rid of those intruders."

Matt reached his hand around the door and tossed the vial onto the floor into the room full of thugs. "Like taking candy from a baby," he said to Monzok and Crystal with a smile. In a few seconds, all was quiet so they entered, holding their breaths.

"Surprise !!!" a voice said as they went inside. It was none other than Sharkey LeGrand. He had pulled his disguise off his head as did the others. There was Stretch, Wilma, and Bobo.

"Hey, what's going on here?" Matt asked totally surprised.

"We had to test you under realistic conditions," Sharkey said. "Sorry for the trickery but we wanted to see how you'd do under real pressure. I'd say you, Crystal, and Monzok, passed with flying colors."

"So that's it," Matt said with a smile. "But what about he gas I just tossed into the room?"

"We substituted it with harmless gas before you left Skytropolis. And as for your BM-88-B, you would have been shooting blanks. Even if you'd shot at us, you couldn't have hurt us."

"Pretty slick," Matt said, "but what about Demonicus Rex?"

"There is no Demonicus Rex," Sharkey explained. "We made that up to create a mission for you. We rented this building on Torvaleda for your little on- the-job training session. But beware, Matt, the next time will be real. No more fooling around. But I'd say you handled yourselves superbly. I'll give a good report to Axis and Locknose. Now get back into your ship and head back to Skytropolis. We already have a real mission for you and your crew and the Cosmic Cobra."

"Thanks for the lesson," Matt said. "That trick neutralizing our invisibility was a real surprise and a shock."

"We couldn't have done it without our own BM-88-B," Sharkey said. "As far as we know, no one else in the galaxy has that capability. But you can't be too careful. Since all BM-88-B weapons are on the same frequency, we simply turned yours off."

"Another lesson, huh?" Crystal stated. "Never take anything for granted."

"We've learned that lesson well today," Matt said with a smile.

"We learned that on many occasions," Bobo and Wilma added.

"I can't wait for the real thing," Matt concluded.